GOTHIC ROMANCE MYSTERY

FLETCHER'S FOLLY

Eileen Lizzie Wells

QVP
Queen Victoria Press

FLETCHER'S FOLLY

ISBN 978-0-9978481-3-7

Queen Victoria Press
153 E. South Street, Ste. 892,
Wooster, OH 44691

In memory of
Gregory Ames

FLETCHER'S FOLLY

Chapter One

The moment I got out of bed I knew the day was going to be different. Looking out of my apartment window, across the Charles River, I could catch the early morning sun glinting on the golden dome of the State House. Off to the right were the John Hancock Tower and the Prudential Center, looking down on the scurrying Bostonians as they hurried in their early morning haste to get to their offices. I felt that I could almost see the work-wheels of the city meshing into gear, ready to start another day of toil and turmoil. The traffic was already heavy on the roads and I could sense the commuters shaking themselves awake as they drove. On the face of it this was just another day, yet – for no obvious reason – I felt it was going to be different.

The only detectable difference I found immediately was that I had overslept. Not that it really mattered . . . I had no job to hurry to and hadn't had one for almost three weeks. At first I had been pleased to find that the little office where I worked – where I typed and filed; filed and typed – was going to close down. Something about the parent company, in San Francisco, concentrating on West Coast operations for the future. I was never over-enthused about my own small part in the company's East Coast operations anyway, so it hardly upset me. But now my one-month's severance pay was coming to an end and it was time to really search in earnest for a new job.

My usual routine was to pick up a copy of the *Globe*, at the corner newsstand, and study the classified ads over coffee and a donut in "The Kambridge Koffeepot," a block-and-a-half down the street. That morning I was in for a disappointment.

"'Morning, Ms. Valentine," said Sid the newsstand man, nodding to me. He seemed somehow a little sheepish; not his usual brash self.

"Good morning, Sid," I said, pushing my long, brown hair back over my shoulder against the wishes of the wind. I looked down at the bare space in front of me. "Where's the *Globe*, Sid?"

That sheepishness again.

"I've, er – I'm sorry, Miss – er, Ms. I'm afraid I'm all out."

"What? You can't be! You've always got a pile here."

It was unbelievable. At this time of day Sid always had quite a stack of newspapers left. Could I be that late? I glanced at the cheap little Timex on my wrist. No, I couldn't be more than twenty minutes later than usual. Strange! However, perhaps that was all the time it took for Sid to sell out his quota. I walked on towards the Koffeepot. What a nuisance, I thought. Now I'll have to wait until I get across into the city and hope to pick up a paper there. But I'd still stop first for my coffee and donut. I brightened at the thought.

Glancing into the little café as I approached the door, I was more than a little annoyed to see that my usual corner table was taken. At this hour the shop was usually almost empty; most of the early morning customers having already hurried off to their offices, their eyes finally opened by their wake-up coffee. As I paused in the doorway, deciding where to sit, the man sitting at "my" table got up and rushed towards me. He pushed roughly past me as though I wasn't even there, was out of the door and then hurrying off down the street. From the brief look I got of him, he seemed to me to be a seedy character and I was glad I had the presence of mind to cling firmly to my pocketbook. Wrong as it may be to make snap decisions about a person's character based solely on their outward appearance, I felt strongly that he was what the novels term a "shady character".

I somewhat modified my thoughts of the man, however, when I went across to now take my usual seat at the corner table. There, lying on the table where the ill-mannered man had left it, was a copy of that morning's *Globe*.

I sat down and picked up the newspaper, mentally deciding that he had left it for me, to atone for his rudeness in pushing past me.

"Good morning, Rebecca. The usual?"

I looked up at Mrs. Edwards's smiling face.

"Yes please, Mrs. E. And take your time," I said. "I'm in no hurry."

The newspaper was already open at the classified section and I turned it over to the *Employment* columns. I seemed to have spent the entire time since I had dropped out of college, three years ago, back in 1970, looking through the employment ads. Of course I knew that wasn't literally true. I'd had jobs in that time . . . lots of jobs! One after another. But they were all what I would term "nothing jobs"! Clerk, typist, file-clerk, receptionist. There had been one interesting one amongst all the others, as secretary to an author. Well, I thought perhaps "secretary" was a little pretentious, especially since the job was only of seven weeks duration. And he wasn't really an actual author either; more of an editor. He was putting together a book made up of other people's articles. I helped him arrange it and did the final typing.

I suppose I was still trying to "find myself". I wanted a job that was *different*. One that was, perhaps, a little unconventional and offered a challenge. I'm sure that being an orphan had a lot to do with these feelings. I needed to establish myself as a real person. All my life I had been shuffled from foster home to foster home; from orphanage to orphanage. Even my name wasn't for real. At least, the Rebecca part was. But not the Valentine. When I was only three I was one of the only survivors of an orphanage fire. All of the orphanage records had been destroyed. Since I was then placed in a new orphanage on St. Valentine's Day, they named me Becky Valentine. I guess I'd come to like it.

Mrs. Edwards brought my coffee and donut and, as I returned to the newspaper, my eye caught a large ad in the center of the Employment section.

Secretary/Companion wanted. Young lady of good education, with

some literary background. Must be competent typist and able to

deal

with correspondence. Unattached, since we are off the beaten track. Live-in as private secretary/companion to lady author. References essential.

I read it again. Could this be it? Could this be the job I had been searching for? *Off the beaten track. Live-in as private secretary-/companion.* It certainly sounded intriguing. There was a salary range mentioned that sounded too good to be true. *Good education, with some literary background.* I wavered. I had had a very mixed education, to say the least. With the many and varied foster homes, I had run the gamut from public school to private school to private tutor and back again. But then, such variety might count in my favor, I thought hopefully. And I had nearly two years of college, until my hard-earned savings had run out and I had to drop out. But then again, while I was there I was majoring in English Literature. And, of course, there was the job I had with the author/editor. I decided it was an opportunity I could not afford to miss. I would write immediately. References were no problem; I had plenty of those from many jobs. And they were all good. One thing I could say for myself was that I was a hard worker. Whatever job I had, and however much I disliked it, I would still do my very best at it. Perhaps now that was going to pay off.

I downed my coffee, determined to go straight back home and write away immediately. I would then do a little grocery shopping, to calm my now vibrant nerves, and relax for the rest of the day. I was planning on going to a movie that evening with Susan Frost. She was my friend from two jobs back. Much like me, she too was searching for an identity. I wondered if she had caught the ad. I could hardly wait for that evening to find out.

"Oh, Becky! It's fantastic! Just what you need."

Susan was immediately enthusiastic, grinning widely as we drove along Church Street in her car. Yet I was beginning to have doubts.

"But that's the trouble," I said. "It's *too* fantastic. Hundreds – no, *thousands* – of girls will be after a job like this. So far as qualifications go, I might be able to scrape by but I'll never be able to compete with the qualifications that most of the others will have."

Susan looked very knowing. "If they are that well qualified, then they've already got good jobs," she said.

I felt better. "Maybe you're right," I said. "But . . . oh, never mind! I guess I'll just be a nervous wreck until I hear from them . . . one way or the other."

Susan parked her little VW Rabbit and we got out and went inside the Kambridge Koffeepot. We always ended up back there for coffee and some final snack after a movie. Then I could walk the block back to my apartment and she could drive straight home.

"I can't understand how come I never saw the ad myself," said Susan, digging into a sundae that screamed calories. "I always go through that paper with a fine-tooth comb, as you know."

"Well, I'm glad you missed it," I said. "Otherwise the odds would have been one more against me."

"Oh, come on, Becky. You'd be ahead of me. I never went to college."

"Well, I only just did." I sucked on my milkshake.

"Where did you say this place is? Vermont, was it?" she asked.

"No. New Hampshire. At least, the post office box number was a New Hampshire one, so I assume that's where the job will be. I looked it up on the map and it's right in the heart of what they call the Lakes Region."

"Oh, you lucky! I hear it's beautiful there. Hey! Perhaps it's on an island in one of the lakes?"

I laughed. "Susan, you're a romantic. Far more likely to be a log cabin at the top of one of the mountains. 'Off the beaten track' they said, remember?"

"So you said. Yes."

"I wish I'd kept the newspaper, or at least cut out the ad, but once I'd written my letter I unthinkingly tossed it away."

"I've got my copy of the *Globe* in the car," said Susan. "Want me to run out and get it?"

"No. Don't bother now, thanks," I said. "Though if you've finished with the paper I would like to take it back to my apartment with me, so I can read it again and dream over it."

"Sure," Susan grunted over her sundae.

We got to talking about the movie we had just seen, which neither of us was enthralled with, and it was nearly a half-hour later that we left the Koffeepot. I got the newspaper from Susan and hurried back to my little apartment.

I had been living there for almost a year and knew that it was going to hurt, leaving it. It had been my first "own home"; all exclusively mine. Before, I had roomed with other girls, but I had always longed for my own place . . . somewhere where I could come and go as I liked, where I could decorate it in my own taste, where I was answerable to no one but myself. And now I was going to give it up.

I had a shower, brushed my teeth and my hair, and got into my pajamas. Sliding into bed, I opened-up Susan's copy of the newspaper and ran my finger down the page of ads. It went all the way to the bottom without stopping. That's funny, I thought. I was sure that was the page the ad had been on. I looked again, and over the page. There was no sign of it.

I checked the rest of the newspaper. Yes, it was the same day and edition that I had. I recognized items of news here and there. I looked carefully through all the *Employment* ads again. No wonder Susan hadn't seen it . . . the job ad – *my* job ad – wasn't there!

Was I going crazy? Had I imagined the whole thing? Yet there was no denying it, the ad was not in this copy of the *Globe*. I got a strange feeling in the pit of my stomach.

Chapter Two

I began to catch glimpses of lakes here and there. As the Trailways bus drove deeper into the heart of New Hampshire's Lakes Region, I started to see how the area had got its name. It was said that you couldn't travel more than fifteen minutes in any direction without coming to a lake. And the lakes were beautiful. Many of them were extremely large having several islands, some with complete houses built on them. I thought back to Susan's remark that I might be bound for just such an island in the middle of a lake. How prophetic she had been.

I was now aware that I was bound for Fletcher Island but all that I knew of it was that it was one of the few still privately-owned islands out somewhere near the middle of the state's largest lake, Lake Winnepesaukee. I loved the sound of that old Native American name and determined to search out its origin and meaning. The lake itself had seventy-two square miles area of water surface; far larger than I could ever imagine. From the maps and travel information I had studied, I knew it also contained more than two hundred and seventy habitable islands. Fletcher was one of these, though exactly where on the lake it was located I had no idea. There was supposed to be a boat waiting to meet my bus, and to take me out to it.

I had never been north of Boston before and was amazed at the beauty of the scenery the farther north I traveled. It was breath-taking, with pines and birches covering the mountains and lowlands like some soft, shaggy carpet, stretching as far as the eye could see. It was late in the fall and I knew I had missed the most spectacular sights of a few weeks earlier. That of the maples and birches, oaks and beeches, in their vivid reds, yellows, oranges, and soft browns, in a great kaleidoscope of blazing colors at the height of the famous Foliage Season. Yet an echo of that glory still remained.

The towns and villages we passed were tucked into this variegated carpet as though apologizing for their intrusion. The blues of the lakes contrasted with the dark greens and browns of the trees, yet complemented them to perfection.

I still found it hard to believe that I actually had the job. I could understand, now, people literally pinching themselves to see if they were awake! The letter had been short but to the point. There was no mention of how many applicants there had been, nor how I had been selected. It simply stated that I had got the job and should arrive on the first bus out of Boston, disembarking at the historic little town of Meredith.

The letterhead had certainly impressed me. It had a coat-of-arms – or so I assumed it to be – in the top left corner: an arm projecting out of the top of a castle tower, with the fist holding a bunch of arrows. At the top right was the address: Fetcher Castle, Fletcher Island, Lake Winnepesaukee. The letter had been signed "John Fletcher". I had almost expected it to say *Sir* John Fletcher, or Lord Fletcher!

Finally the bus pulled into Meredith, stopping right opposite the docks. With my two suitcases, I got down and gratefully stretched my legs. As the bus pulled away, I crossed to the docks and looked about me. The only boat tied-up there was an ancient, though obviously seaworthy, sightseeing boat bearing a banner encouraging tourists to "see the fabulous foliage from the water." Surely an opportunity not to be missed, I thought . . . except that the foliage season was very definitely at an end and the last of the tourists must have long since fled south from the approaching winter. I sat down on my suitcases and waited.

Fifteen or twenty minutes passed with no sign of any other boat. I got up, realizing that I was very cold, and walked along the dock. As I approached the sightseeing boat I was surprised to find that there were indeed some half-dozen or so hardy tourists aboard, and apparently willing to take the trip around the lake. They sat huddled in the middle of the boat, bundled up in their thick coats and scarves, determined to catch the dregs of the fading autumn.

"See the foliage, miss? Still beautiful from the lake, y'know."

I smiled at the enthusiasm of the boat's skipper as he climbed up out of the vessel and approached me with his ever-hopeful sales pitch.

"Thanks but no thanks," I said. "I'm supposed to be met here by a private boat."

He half-turned and looked out over the lake, squinting into the bright, if unwarm, reflected sunlight. I followed his gaze and saw the vast expanse of empty, ruffled water. No sign of any craft. He moved back towards his boat.

"Okay, miss. But we push off in fifteen minutes, if you should change your mind."

I thanked him and headed towards a little snack bar at the head of the docks. A good cup of coffee would be welcome, I decided. The waters of the lake still looked beautiful this time of year, when viewed from the window of a heated bus, but up close from a wind-blown dock was something else.

Ten minutes later, after coffee and a delicious hot-dog, I prepared to go back to the dock. But I could see from the snack bar window that there was still no sign of any other craft, anywhere out on the lake.

"Where's the boat coming from, that's to pick you up?" asked the lady behind the cash register, as I paid my bill.

"Fletcher Island," I said.

"Fletcher? Fletcher?" She frowned. "Don't know that I know Fletcher. Of course, I'm fairly new here myself." She turned to a large, framed map hanging on the wall behind her. Her finger moved around it before stopping somewhere near the center of the lake. "Ah! Here it is. Oh, that's a long way off! Are you sure they said to come to Meredith?"

I nodded.

"That's strange," she said. "Of course I'm no sailor, but I would have thought Gilford would have been much closer to it. We're all the way down here, at the end of the lake, see?" She pointed.

I didn't need to check the letter to confirm that I had been directed to Meredith. I had read it a dozen times or more and could see it plainly, now, in my mind's eye. But where was the boat to meet me?

They knew what time the bus got in, and it was on time. Why hadn't they come? What was I to do?

"Why don't you get old Red to give you a lift out there?" suggested the helpful snack bar lady, nodding towards the sightseeing boat.

"Do you think he would?" I asked.

"Sure. 'Course, he might want you to buy half a ticket or something." She chuckled. "But I guess that would be worth it."

I agreed, thanked her, and hurried out.

"Give you a lift to your island? Don't see why not," said Red, the skipper, when I approached him. "Which island is it?" He lifted his cap to scratch his balding head.

"Fletcher," I replied.

His face dropped. He stopped in the middle of his scratch as though suddenly frozen. Then, slowly, he replaced his cap, never moving his eyes from mine. He didn't say a word and, for a moment, I wondered if he had heard me. Then he turned away and started casting off the lines holding the boat to the dock.

"Er, sorry, miss. No." He spoke with his back now turned to me. "We're not allowed to deviate from our set course. Sorry."

I was dumbfounded. He had seemed so friendly and easy-going, so willing to be helpful just a moment before. Why the sudden change, I wondered.

"But . . . you said . . ."

"I'm sorry, miss. I made a mistake."

Chapter Three

He looked at me sideways, and studied me for a moment. He must have seen my bewilderment, my frustration and despair. For a moment the old captain softened.

"So, Fletcher's Folly, is it? You really want to go there?"

"I have to," I said. "I have nowhere else to go."

"Aye."

He seemed to think hard for a moment and then seemed to come to a decision. He pointed to the boat. "Get aboard, miss," he said. "I won't – I can't – take you to Fletcher but I'll tell you what I'll do. There's another island not too far from it: Egypt Island. I'll take you there. There's some young fellas been campin' there for the summer. I think they're still there. They've got a boat. P'raps you can get one of them to take you across to Fletcher?"

"Oh, thank you! Thank you very much, captain."

I was relieved and, as we moved away from the dock, heading into the not-so-calm waters of the lake, I saw he was almost his original self again. But still I wondered what had caused that sudden change. Surely it couldn't have just been the name Fletcher?

Why had the old boat captain referred to the island as Fletcher's *Folly*? I turned up the collar of my coat against the cool breeze and tried to concentrate my thoughts on the beauty of the scenery we were passing.

It took over an hour to get out to Egypt Island, though I don't suppose we took the most direct route. The captain turned out to be an excellent tour guide and, despite the lackluster of the foliage, he made the trip interesting by pointing out and commenting on the many points of interest that we passed along the way. Eventually I saw that we were approaching an island that was dominated by a large, pyramid-shaped hill, though it seemed more like a mountain seen from the level of the water. Obviously this was Egypt Island. The boat slowed and, despite the turbulence, the captain brought it gently alongside a well-constructed dock sticking out into the lake from the base of the pyramid-hill.

"So far, so good, young lady," said the old man, as he handed me ashore and passed my bags after me. "Now you take care, d'you hear? Sure you won't change your mind and go the whole tour with us?"

I smiled down at his obviously-worried face. "Thank you captain. You've been very kind. I do appreciate it. But no, I have to go on to Fletcher Island."

He again looked hard at me, without speaking. I felt vaguely uneasy. Then, shaking his head, he turned back to the boat, cast off, and headed once more out into the lake. For a moment I felt tempted to shout after him; to ask him to come back for me. I felt a sudden urge to get back to the mainland, back home to my secure little apartment in Cambridge. But that was ridiculous! I had given up the apartment and, besides, I *wanted* this job. I had been longing for something different, hadn't I?

"Hello there! Are you sure you're in the right place?"

I jumped.

"Sorry. Didn't mean to startle you."

I turned to meet a fair-haired, sun-tanned, young man, with clear blue eyes and a wide, friendly smile. He must have been about twenty – a couple of years younger than me – and was quite handsome. He was dressed in faded jeans and a thick fisherman's sweater topped by a bright red windbreaker. His once-white sneakers had a splash of yellow paint on the left foot. I couldn't help but smile back at him.

"That's all right," I said. "It's me who should apologize, for invading your island uninvited like this."

He rubbed his hands on his jeans, picked up my suitcases, and started to lead the way off the dock and on to the island.

"You're lucky you caught me," he said. "I'm the last one here. All the others have already left. I was just finishing closing-up the place. Ten minutes later and you'd have found the island deserted."

I gasped. Supposing I *had* missed him? I would have been stranded out there in the middle of the lake, all alone.

"My name's Simon," went on the young man. "I didn't know anyone else was renting this place after us. Bit late in the season, isn't it?"

"No. No, I'm not staying here," I said. I introduced myself and went on to explain my problem and how the captain had suggested I might get a ride across to Fletcher Island from there. Simon seemed very easy-going and happy to oblige.

"Oh, sure thing Rebecca . . . er, Rebecca or Becky?"

"Becky will do fine," I said, breathing easier.

"Okay, Becky. Then just give me a couple of minutes and we'll be all set." He looked at the lake. "Getting rough. A bit choppy. We'll be all right though. Nothing we can't handle."

I really liked Simon. He seemed so capable and accepted my sudden appearance in the most casual way, as though strangers dropped in on him every day. I rather wished there had been more time. I would have enjoyed having him show me about the place.

He finished locking-up an A-frame summerhouse where, as he explained, he and five other boys had spent the previous two and a half months. They were all from New York and had been coming there every year for the past three years. I asked him what he knew of Fletcher Island.

"Not as much as I should, I guess." He grinned. "Considering how many times I'm been here. We spend our time swimming, fishing, and sailing out on the water. We study a little and go out to all the attractions around the lake. Time seems to fly."

"Is there actually a real castle on Fletcher Island?" I asked a little hesitantly.

"Sure thing. In fact that's why they call it 'Fletcher's Folly'."

"What do you mean?"

"Well, it's a copy of an old medieval castle like they have in Europe, only a lot smaller of course. But the guy who built it ran out of money, so it's only half finished. *Ergo*, Fletcher's Folly."

I laughed. "I see. And are the Fletchers who live there now, descendants of the original would-be builder?"

He shrugged. "I guess so. But I don't really know. You say you're going to work there, Becky?"

"Yes." I told him all about the ad and my excitement about getting the job. He didn't enthuse, as I thought he would.

"I suppose it's okay," he said hesitantly. "I mean, I can see how great it seems, and all. But still . . ." He looked at me, suddenly serious. "You know, you should be careful about running off to some deserted place, to work for people you've never met and know nothing about."

I was touched by his concern and squeezed his arm. "Thank you, Simon. You're sweet. But as you say, the Fletchers have been here for a long time, so I'm sure they're respectable."

"Sure!" He smiled again, the frown disappearing from his face. "Didn't mean to scare you or anything. Yes, I'm sure the Fletchers are solid, upstanding citizens. Shall we go?"

He took up my bags again and we returned to the dock, where I then saw an outboard-engined dinghy was tethered. The little blue boat took us around the end of Egypt Island and, as we cleared the head, I got my first view of Fletcher Island. It was quite large and well covered with trees. There were a lot of pines, with a generous scattering of oaks and maples, plus a few white birches. From that distance I could just make out the top of the castle in the center of the island. As I was to learn later, it was built on rising ground that allowed the windows of the upper floors to look out over the treetops. The castle was not as large as I had imagined, though truly I didn't know what to expect. It was certainly impressive.

There were grim, castellated battlements and one large, imposing, tower at one corner. Much smaller towers were at two of the other corners, though one of these was incomplete. Where I expected to see a second large tower there was nothing. The castle was built of native New Hampshire granite and, as such, blended into the island as though it had grown up from it naturally. The granite gave the castle a timelessness, such that one could well believe it to have been the actual scene of numerous battles and sieges. I could almost image I could see distant figures walking the battlements, the dying sun glinting on their helmets and chainmail. For a moment I thought that I did indeed catch a glimpse of someone or something on top of the main tower; something glinting in the fading light. But then it was gone.

The ground floor of the castle was hidden behind the trees but, from our position out on the lake, I could see the windows of the upper floors. They were small and spaced evenly along the walls, set into the stonework and showing the thickness of the granite. The windows of the third and top floors were in the style of arrow slits, such as I saw in the towers. I couldn't help but think how dull and gloomy those rooms must be. I wondered if the castle had the traditional dungeons, but knowing of the granite base on which it was built I doubted that the Fletchers' penchant for realism extended that far.

As we drew closer neither Simon nor I spoke. I felt a sense of awe as my eyes remained fixed on those dark, gray battlements. Somehow the castle lacked the impressive Crusaders-for-God-and-Right appeal that I had hoped to find. With a shudder I realized that it brought more to mind the Dracula brand of chateau!

Who would want to build such a place, out here on this beautiful lake, in this idyllic setting? What sort of person had the Fletcher been who had set about this monumental task? He must have been driven by a tremendous urge; a great desire to emulate his ancestors. But was that a noble desire . . . or was it madness? Certainly it had turned out to be financial madness. I couldn't even imagine the money it must have cost to create such a monstrous building. And to think that I was going to live in that place. I had committed myself, freely, to incarceration!

I shivered. It wasn't really cold, yet I felt an unusual chill creeping over me as we drew nearer. What was it about the castle that should affect me this way? Why, despite the beauty of the lake and of the other islands, did Fletcher Island suddenly seem to me to be . . . forbidding? Yes, that was the word. Forbidding.

Chapter Four

"We'll go around the island to the right, counterclockwise," said Simon, bringing the little boat around. "I don't know exactly where the dock would be so we'll just have to go around till we come to it.'

"Fine," I replied.

It seemed strangely quiet. Neither of us spoke much. The noise of the little engine sounded almost profane in the monastic silence that seemed to encompass the island. Perhaps it was just that we had come into shelter from the wind, or perhaps the wind had dropped? Whatever the reason, it seemed as quiet as – the word came naturally, and frighteningly – as quiet as the grave.

I looked up at the trees that towered above us as we followed the shoreline. I couldn't see the castle from where we were, for which I was glad. Peering in towards shore, I found that the trees were so densely packed together it was like a jungle, making it quite impossible to see through them. The shoreline was rock and boulder; huge slabs of granite that would make it impossible to land at any spot other than a prepared dock. When I looked down into the water, I could see great jagged rocks below the surface. Simon had become aware of these and throttled back the engine, slowing to half speed.

"There it is!"

I looked up and saw a short, floating dock against the shore. Behind it I could see what looked like an overgrown footpath disappearing into the darkness of the trees. I shivered to think that I'd have to go along it.

"There's no other boat here," I said. "Do you think they went to Meredith for me after all, and I missed them?"

Simon juggled with the business of tying-up at the dock before answering. The water was getting rough and the dinghy was bouncing backwards and forwards, making it difficult to connect. The sun had disappeared behind a mass of dark, ominous clouds.

"My guess is, this is a secondary dock. Probably used only once in a while. Sort of a Tradesmen's Entrance. There's probably another major one farther around."

He helped me out of the boat and we got my bags ashore. I started to thank him but he held up his hand.

"Hold it." He grinned. "We're not parting just yet. I can't just leave you here and take off. The very least I can do is see you safely up to the house . . . sorry, castle."

I almost hugged him.

That the Tradesmen's Path was seldom used quickly became obvious. We struggled along, each with a suitcase, stepping over fallen branches and forcing our way through dense underbrush. The trail led uphill and soon I was puffing and panting. Suddenly, quite unexpectedly, we stepped out onto clear ground not twenty feet from the imposing walls of the castle itself. Simon pointed.

"There. Just to the right. There's a door."

You could almost miss it. The bare wood of the door, and its frame, was weathered gray and blended in with the color of the surrounding stonework. We went up to it.

"Doesn't look as though it's been opened in years," I said. "Are you sure this place is inhabited, Simon?"

He flashed his cheering smile. "You're the one who got the letter from here, remember?"

I laughed. "You're right. As you said, this must be the old Tradesmen's Entrance. Let's walk around and see if we can find the front door."

"Good idea."

Simon leading the way, we started off following the wall to the right. By then the sky had become quite overcast and it was obvious that a storm was on its way. We reached a corner and, as we turned it, Simon suddenly stopped dead in his tracks, throwing up an arm to stop me.

"What is it? What's wrong?"

He pointed to the ground in front of me. There, right where we would have stepped, was a savage-looking bear trap. Its vicious jaws were set open. One false step and those saw-teeth would snap closed, penetrating to the very bone. I shuddered and looked about me.

"Do you think there are bears about here, Simon?"

He shook his head. "Not on the island, no. I'd very much doubt it. I've never heard of any beyond the mainland. I think it's far more likely that this was set for human prowlers. Trespassers."

"How horrid!"

Going carefully around the trap, we moved on. We now walked much slower and kept our eyes on the ground. Finally, as we rounded another corner, we came to the front of the castle.

"Civilization!" muttered Simon. I hoped he was right.

We could see an imposing entranceway ahead of us and, to the right, a reasonably well-kept pathway leading down the hill to a large dock and boathouse.

"Well, at least there's no moat and drawbridge to cross," he added, as we climbed the half-dozen stone steps up to the imposing front doors.

I glanced up above me and caught my breath. "What's that, Simon?"

He looked up to where I pointed.

"Wow! They don't need a drawbridge; they've got a portcullis."

"A port what?"

"Portcullis," he explained. "See, it's like a huge iron gate suspended over the entrance. It can be dropped down to protect the gateway from unwanted visitors."

I eyed the fierce metal points projecting down, and tried not to think of it dropping accidentally. "They certainly don't encourage strangers," I said, forcing myself to be calm. "Thank goodness I've got a letter of introduction."

We put down my bags and Simon raised the great, bronze, lion-headed knocker on one of the double doors. As he let it fall, the boom it created seemed to echo through the whole of the castle.

"Guess they should hear that," he quipped. "Loud enough to wake the dead."

I grimaced and studied the doors. They were huge; perhaps eight feet high. Made of solid oak beams, they were strapped with thick, black, bands of iron and supported by huge iron hinges elaborately shaped like animal claws. Set in the stonework, above the doors, was the same design I had found on the letter. The Fletcher's coat-of-arms: a human arm projecting from a tower, its fist clutching a handful of arrows.

I was startled when the right hand door suddenly swung open, silently, on well-oiled hinges. I smiled to myself when I realized I had been expecting them to creak.

Facing us was a tall, remarkably handsome man. He must have been in his late thirties but the small, neat mustache and the hint of gray at the temples of his fine, dark hair made him appear older. He was wearing a deep purple, velvet-faced, smoking jacket . . . the sort I'd seen only in movies. He had thick, very red lips and slightly bushy eyebrows from beneath which his striking gray eyes rapidly appraised us. The aquiline nose added to his aristocratic appearance. His brow furrowed slightly.

"Mr. Fletcher?" I asked.

He nodded, his gaze rapidly sweeping over me from head to toe.

I forced what I hoped was an endearing smile. "I - I'm Miss Valentine. Rebecca Valentine. You – you're expecting me?"

The frown deepened for a moment, then cleared.

"Why, Miss Valentine. Of course." His voice was deep and musical. "We weren't expecting you until tomorrow."

"Oh!" I faltered. "But your letter said today. The fifteenth."

The frown returned momentarily then, once again, cleared. "Today is the fifteenth? Do forgive me!" He shrugged his shoulders helplessly. "You see now why we need you . . . why my sister needs a secretary? We get very much out of touch, here on the island." A thought seemed to strike him. "But however did you get here? I sent no boat for you today, of course."

Greatly relieved at the simple explanation for my not having been met, I introduced Simon and explained how he had been good enough to bring me there.

"That was indeed kind of you," said Mr. Fletcher. He stepped forward and took up my bags. "But we must not now detain you, Simon. The weather is turning for the worst. You had best be off right away."

As Simon was about to reply the sky opened up and, with a crack of thunder so loud that it nearly caused me to jump into my new employer's arms, down came the rain in torrents.

"Perhaps we'd better get inside?" I suggested.

We were protected in the entranceway but, as the wind got up, the rain began to invade the threshold.

"Yes. Yes, of course."

It seemed to me that Mr. Fletcher was almost reluctant to let Simon into the castle, but he obviously had no choice. This feeling was strengthened when he delayed inside the doors, looking out at the rapidly worsening weather.

"I wonder if it's going to clear again," he said. "You must be anxious to be on your way, Simon."

Simon seemed not to have noticed the implications.

"Oh, don't worry about me, Mr. Fletcher," he said cheerily. "I have no special schedule to keep. Looks like the storm's set for the night now, anyway."

"Yes. Yes, I'm afraid you may be right."

Mr. Fletcher closed the great door and, leaving my bags sitting on the floor there, led the way down the dark main hallway towards a half-open door through which light streamed.

The hallway itself was extremely gloomy and ill lit. As we passed along it, I could vaguely make out heavily wainscoted walls bearing old oil paintings. A huge stairway disappeared up into the blackness off to the right. I could scarcely make out the high ceiling above. It seemed to be domed and heavily beamed, but so high I could see no details. Passageways struck off into the darkness on either side of the open door. On the wall opposite the staircase hung an imposing array of shields, swords, and battle-axes, the light from the room we approached glinting dully on them. I was surprised to notice, in the half-light, that they seemed to be covered with a fine layer of dust.

Following Mr. Fletcher through the doorway, we found ourselves in a small sitting room. I was happy to see a welcoming fire burning in the big, stone fireplace. The room was comfortably furnished with a settee and two large armchairs. There was also a small table with two straight-back chairs drawn up to it, a heavily carved, antique sideboard, a bureau, and a long, low coffee-table. From the high, ornately-decorated ceiling hung a chandelier. It was one of the old types, holding actual lit candles rather than electric light bulbs.

"Oh," I said, gazing up at it. "Did the storm knock out your electricity, Mr. Fletcher?"

He followed the direction of my gaze.

"No, Miss Valentine." He smiled. "We have no electricity here on Fletcher Island."

"You mean . . . none at all?" Stupidly my jaw dropped open in amazement.

"No. None at all." His smile widened.

I pulled myself together, feeling the beginnings of a blush starting in my cheeks. How stupid of me. Obviously an island, way out in the middle of a lake as large as Winnepesaukee, would be extremely unlikely to have electricity. I should have thought of that before. I glanced at him, caught the humor in his eyes and felt the blush deepen. I quickly lowered my eyes and told myself to stop acting like a schoolgirl. I also thought to myself how remarkably handsome he looked when he smiled like that. Perhaps there would be some recompense for working and living in such archaic surroundings.

"You must be hungry." He interrupted my thoughts. "I'll see about getting you both something to eat and then I'm sure you'll be wanting to get an early night after your travels."

He disappeared through a little door to one side of the fireplace. I had not noticed it before.

"Well, this is very nice."

Simon plumped himself down in one of the armchairs beside the fireplace and looked about him at the room.

"It's certainly comfortable," I said, sinking thankfully on to the settee.

I suddenly realized how very tired I was. It was probably due to a combination of the long bus ride, the uncertainty at the Meredith docks, and then the frustrations and nervous excitement of the journey across to the castle. I was decidedly hungry, now that food had been mentioned, but I knew that I would be equally happy to get to bed. I wondered what the next day would bring. Would I then meet Cynthia Fletcher, my actual boss? What sort of work would I be required to do? Would my duties bring me into any personal contact with Mr. . . . with John Fletcher, I wondered? I had to admit, I rather hoped they might.

Chapter Five

I thought I would fall asleep as soon as my head touched the pillow, but I was wrong. Whether it was the excitement of the day, the rumbling and crashing of the thunder, or the strangeness of my room, I don't know. Whatever the reason, I found myself lying there weary yet wide-awake.

The Fletchers had certainly spared no expense in the furnishing of their castle . . . which may have helped explain why they ran out of money. The bed in which I lay was a four-poster. Not a modern replica but an original; three or four hundred years old. Like most of the furniture in the castle it must have been brought here from Europe. I had to admit, it was remarkably comfortable.

At the foot of the bed was an old blanket chest as old as, if not older than, the bed itself. There was a bedside table on which stood a candleholder and candle. Against the wall was a huge, elaborately carved wardrobe in which I had hung my meager selection of skirts and dresses. Beside the door sat a bachelor chest, a three-branched candelabra on top of it alongside a non-working though very elegant-looking Victorian clock. There was an armchair, an unpretentious little dressing table, and a quilt-topped chest built in as a window seat, to complete the furnishings. Small, but comfortable, I thought.

On first exploring the room I had received one delightful surprise. There was a tiny door in the far corner of the room. I opened it expecting to find a dismal little closet. Imagine my surprise to discover that it led into a wonderful, modern, private bathroom. Perhaps the Fletchers weren't so crazy after all.

I lay there in the great bed, looking around again at the furniture as the room was periodically lit by the recurring flashes of lightning. My room was at the back of the castle, on the second floor. Not too far away, to my left, were the servants' quarters, through a locked door in the passageway that separated them from the family quarters. The servants had their own stairway up the small North Tower. The Fletchers themselves had a suite on the ground floor, at the front of the castle in the eastern corner. Alongside their rooms rose the great East Tower. Impressive, it rose high above the rest of the castle. I determined to explore it at some future date. The view of the lake, from the top, must be truly fantastic, I thought. Little did I realize, then, what that imposing East Tower held in store for me.

To my surprise, and slight apprehension, Simon had been given a room for the night at the front of the building, towards the south corner. It was some considerable distance from mine, through a seeming maze of corridors. Mr. Fletcher had explained that, not expecting guests, it was the only room suitable. Seeing the number of doors off the upstairs passageway, presumably all bedrooms, I couldn't quite understand why one would be more suitable than another. With my still unsteady nerves, I would much have preferred that Simon be within easy reach should I need him. Yet, why would I need him?

　　As if in answer to my thoughts I heard a sudden scuffling in the far corner of the room. I sat up. The sound came again. With a sudden flash of lightning I saw the two bright little eyes of a tiny mouse. He looked even more frightened than I felt. I laughed out loud, and heard him scamper away. I didn't really mind little mice but decided I would ask Mr. Fletcher if he couldn't do something to keep them out of my bedroom.

　　I had just snuggled down again beneath the covers when I heard a tapping sound. It seemed to be coming from the direction of the bathroom. I held my breath and listened. Yes, it came again, much louder this time. Certainly no mouse. I peered towards the bathroom door, but no lightning came to show me what might be there. For what seemed an age I lay there, scarcely daring to breathe. Every once in a while the tapping would sound again. Suddenly I sat bolt upright in my bed. A scream! I was sure I had heard a scream. I strained my ears.

　　Nothing. Then, again the tapping. Making as much noise as possible, I struck a match and lit the bedside candle. A glance at my watch, lying on the table, told me it was already nearly two o'clock in the morning. I slipped out of the high bed and found my slippers. Throwing my robe over my shoulders, and with the candle held high, I crossed the room to the bathroom and stood with my hand on the doorknob. I waited. The knocking came again, definitely from inside. Screwing up my courage, I turned the knob and threw open the door.

　　There was no one inside. I don't know whether I was relieved or disappointed. I certainly don't know what I would have done if there had been someone there. As I looked about me the knocking suddenly came again. It was much louder in the bathroom and I laughed when I realized what it was. Despite the modern appearance of the bathroom, the water pipes, beneath the washbasin, were exposed and they vibrated against the edges of the holes where they disappeared through the far wall. I remembered once experiencing a similar fright, for the very same reason, in an old apartment in Boston. I had been told that it was something to do with the hot water. Thankfully, and wearily, I turned once more towards the bed. It was then I heard the scream again.

It was difficult to judge the direction from which the scream came. The wind outside was still high and, with the occasional rumble of thunder, it was impossible to pinpoint the direction. I went to the door of my room and stood, with my head against the crack, listening. Apart from the odd night-creaks of the house, all seemed still. Had I imagined it? What with the mouse and then the water pipes, my nerves were certainly on edge. Should I ignore it? But I knew I would never sleep a wink that night if I did. I determined to go and find Simon.

I turned the door handle and pulled. Nothing happened. I pulled harder. The door was stuck. Stuck . . . or locked? Was I ever getting paranoid, I told myself. How ridiculous! Why ever would anyone lock me in my room? I held the candle close to the door handle and peered through the crack. My heart skipped a beat. Plainly I could see the bar of brass. I was locked in.

The lock was one of the big, old-fashioned, brass ones with a huge keyhole. Obviously, I told myself (not really believing it) that it was simply old and worn and had locked itself due to vibration. Why, there wasn't even a key in the lock, at least not on my side of the door. Peering through the crack, all was black but I was sure there was no key on the other side either. I looked about for something with which to try to force it open. The only possibility seemed to be the candle snuffer on the bedside table. It was brass with a long, cast-iron handle. The end of the handle had been curved around to facilitate hanging it from a hook but at some time in its life it had been dropped and the main part of the curl had broken off. The remaining curved section might just do the job, I thought. I took it across to the door and gingerly inserted it into the lock. A little jiggling about, together with the fact that the lock *was* old and worn, finally brought about the "click" I had been wanting. I turned the handle and opened the door.

I put on my robe properly and fastened it securely about me. Taking the three-branched candelabra, and feeling a little like a heroine in a Gothic novel, I set off purposefully down the corridor in what I hoped was the direction of Simon's room. As I passed the top of the main staircase I paused and leaned over the bannister rail, listening. Not a sound; all was still. By then I was sure that there was a logical explanation for the scream. Surely, I reasoned, if it had been real then others would have heard it and would be investigating. But then, perhaps everybody else was asleep. I had heard it only because I happened to be awake.

Perhaps it was just the way the wind howled through a piece of stonework? Or perhaps it was a hoot-owl . . . though they would surely hoot, wouldn't they, not scream? Or did I mean a screech-owl? Did they have them in New Hampshire?

I came to the end of the corridor and turned left. I was pretty certain that I would then be heading towards the south front of the castle. Suddenly, ahead of me, I saw a light. The corridor made another turn to the left and, just beyond the turn, there was a room with its door open. That would be Simon's room, I thought, and quickened my pace. Perhaps he had heard the scream too and was on his way to see me.

I turned the bend and, sure enough, found an open door. A candelabra similar to the one I carried burned on top of a chest of drawers just inside the room. It was obviously Simon's room – I recognized his windbreaker thrown casually over a chair back – but the room was empty. As I stood there looking about me and wondering what to do, I noticed Simon's sneakers lying on the floor, tucked under the side of the bed. Why would he have gone off without his shoes, I wondered? If he had gone to investigate the screams surely he would have put on his shoes. And what about the candles? He wouldn't be wandering about this strange, forbidding castle in his stockinged feet and without a light, surely.

The storm seemed to have died down and I went across to the window on the far side of the room. I parted the heavy drapes a fraction and peered out. The storm had moved on over to the White Mountains and I could see the intermittent flashes of lightning way off in the distance. The wind had finally dropped and the moon was struggling to show itself through the threadbare clouds.

My eyes were caught by a movement down below me. A figure of some sort, surely? Simon's room was at the front of the castle, towards the south corner, where the great South Tower was yet to be built.

Looking down to my left I could just make out the stone boathouse and the dock beside it. It was on the dock that I saw something move. As I strained my eyes, the moon made a brief appearance and I saw a strange sight. It looked like a man with his head all bound up in bandages. He was lifting a bulky, and obviously heavy, bundle into a small rowboat. The moon was veiled again and some minutes passed before I could relocate the strange figure. By then it – he? – had rowed some distance out on to the lake. The water had calmed considerably with the passing of the storm, but the little dinghy bearing the figure still bounced about a lot. In the next brief flood of moonlight the man with the bandaged head stood up in the boat and for a moment I thought he had fallen overboard. There was certainly a splash.

A short time later, with the next parting of the clouds, I saw the man was still there, though now rowing back towards the castle. I thought it strange that anyone should be out in a boat at that time of night, especially so soon after the storm, but then a supposed it must be a fisherman; perhaps one of the Fletchers' servants. I vaguely remember someone having once said that the fish bite well after rain. I turned away from the window.

After a final look around, I started back to my own room. If Simon wanted to be wandering around a strange castle at night, with no light and no shoes, then that was up to him. I was finally feeling very tired and was sure I'd have no further trouble getting to sleep. It seemed obvious I must have imagined the screams. Who the night-fisherman was should be no concern of mine. All I wanted to do now was get back to my bed and go to sleep. I'd see Simon in the morning.

When I finally got back to my room, on an impulse I took the candle snuffer and relocked the door. I doubted that anyone *had* deliberately locked me in my room but, just in case, there was no reason for them to know that I could still get out and about.

Chapter Six

I was awakened by a repeated tapping on my bedroom door. At first, in my drowsy state, I thought it was the bathroom pipes again. Then I realized what it was and, rubbing the sleep from my eyes, I called "Come in."

The door opened to reveal a young servant girl balancing a breakfast tray on her knee. She got a good grip on it and came into the room to put it down on the bedside table. I saw then that she was not as young as I had first imagined. She was short and slight and her face was thin and lined. The whole left side of the face was a deep reddish-brown from a birthmark. The shape was not unlike the shape of a human hand so that my first thought was that someone had struck her with considerable force. On realizing it to be a birthmark, I quickly revised my thinking.

I sat up in bed and smiled at her. She looked back at me, her face an expressionless mask.

"Thank you very much," I said. "I'm Becky. What's your name?"

She stood there, silent, as though I had not spoken. I took her to be about fifty years of age and under-nourished. I tried again, this time pointing to myself and then to her. She continued to regard me in silence for a while then she bobbed a curtsey and hurried out of the room, closing the door behind her. It was only then that I realized that the door was no longer locked.

Had it ever been locked? Had I imagined it all; the scream and the visit to Simon's room? Was it all a dream? Seeing the candle snuffer lying on top of the bachelor chest, next to the door, I knew it had been real.

Glancing at my watch I saw that I had slept much later than I had meant to. With the night's excursions I suppose it was not surprising, but I didn't want to give my new employer the wrong impression . . . My new employer! I thought of John Fletcher as I had first met him. So tall! He must be a little over six feet, I thought. Certainly tall to my modest five feet five. I was not sure whether or not I cared for his mustache. It certainly made him look very distinguished, but I couldn't help thinking of all the villains in the movies who had mustaches.

What was I doing? Here I was idly day-dreaming about Mr. Fletcher as though he was some . . . some heart-throb! I should be up and dressed by now, I told myself. I jumped out of bed and hurried into the bathroom. The breakfast could wait.

"Ah! Miss Valentine. And looking delightful, if I may say so. Good morning to you. Did you sleep well?"

"Good morning," I said. John Fletcher greeted me at the bottom of the grand staircase. Could he have been waiting for me?

"Yes." I felt a little white lie was in order. "I slept beautifully."
Actually once I *did* get to sleep I had slept soundly through until I was
awakened, so it was not really a lie.

I noticed that Mr. Fletcher was "elegantly casual". He wore fine-
tailored, tan-colored slacks above comfortable-looking brown suede
loafers. His shirt was a dark green, silk print with a yellow cravat tucked
into the neck. His smile made me feel good and I was glad I had chosen
to dress up a little, rather than to just throw on a shirt and jeans. I
couldn't help noticing his approving glance at my full, blue skirt and the
plain white blouse I had chosen. Businesslike, I had thought as I had
slipped it on, yet becoming.

"The storm certainly cleared the air," he said by way of
conversation, as he led the way into the little sitting room we had been
in the previous evening. "The sun is out and it promises to be a beautiful
day."

I felt good. It had obviously been the long journey, the weather,
and the general uncertainty that had unnerved me the day before.

"Will I be meeting your sister this morning, Mr. Fletcher?" I asked.

He stopped, his hand on the sitting room door. "Oh, yes. In fact we
are about to do so right now. By the way, I would like you to call me
John; my sister, Cynthia. We shall call you Rebecca."

His smile struck me again and I felt a little light-headed as I
followed him into the room.

"Cynthia, this is Rebecca. I told you she arrived late yesterday."

For a moment I thought it was an old woman seated at the
fireplace. When she turned to look at me, however, I saw that she was

probably only five years or so older than John. Her hair was dyed what was probably intended to be a vibrant silver but, through some misapplication, it had turned out a dull gray with ugly yellowish tinges. A cigarette with a long ash, stuck in a long, black holder, hung from the corner of her mouth. Splotches of ash, on her rumpled black dress, showed that she was apt to forget that she was smoking. Her face showed lines beneath the heavily-applied pancake makeup. Here eyelashes were heavy with mascara. Diamonds – or so I assumed them to be – flashed on her fingers but did not detract from the broken, chipped, red-painted fingernails. She looked at me out of tired, heavy-lidded eyes, the pupils a watery gray.

"Julie?" she said.

"No. *Rebecca*," John emphasized. He looked at me. "You'll find Cynthia's a little slow first thing in the morning."

"Slow, nothing!" snorted Cynthia, suddenly vibrant. "Let's get to work." She stood up.

"Oh, Mr. Fletcher . . . John. What about Simon? I would like to thank him for bringing me here, before he leaves this morning. Is he about yet?"

John and Cynthia exchanged glances and then John headed for the little door beside the fireplace. "I'm afraid you're too late, Rebecca," he said, without looking back. "When the storm died down last night – about midnight, I think it was – Simon decided he'd take off then. It seems there was some early morning appointment he had previously forgotten about. Didn't want to be late for it." He disappeared through the door, closing it behind him.

"But . . ." I was about to say that I had seen Simon's jacket and shoes in his room nearly two hours after midnight. I bit my tongue. Something was wrong.

"Come along, child."

Cynthia swept past me to the main sitting room door through which I had entered. I hated to be called "child". I had disliked it when I was a teenager but had then had to accept it. Now that I was twenty-two I felt I didn't have to.

"The name's Rebecca," I said, pointedly.

Cynthia took not the slightest notice. She led the way out into the hall and, with a shrug, I followed.

"We'll go into the study. That's where I do my work." Cynthia turned right along the passageway, and then into the first door on the left.

The study was very pleasant. It had the dark mahogany wainscoting I had noticed in the entrance hall on my arrival. But where the hallway's paneling had gone up the wall as far as I could see, in the semi-dark of yesterday, the study was only paneled halfway. Above that the walls were covered with rich, red, velour-patterned wallpaper that gave the room a pleasant warmth. The high ceiling was of rough, white plaster crossed by the heavy oak beams found in all the rooms of the castle. There were large casement windows, with diamond-paned, leaded glass, looking out over the green lawn that spread down the hill to the lakefront. The furniture was much as I was to find throughout the castle: a conglomeration of widely varying periods, though all beautiful, genuine antiques.

A breakfront library bookcase, which I thought might be Hepplewhite, covered half of one wall. It was crammed with books, mostly modern novels and innumerable paperbacks. Next to it stood a Queen Anne bureau, its flap down and holding an   incongruously modern typewriter. A large refectory table filled most of the center of the room. Its bulbous, ornately-carved legs told me it was Elizabethan. Almost certainly an original. There was a wide variety of chairs about the room, a couple of small card tables, and a Victorian roll-top desk which I soon learned was Cynthia's. All horizontal surfaces were covered with reams of paper: typewriter manuscripts, envelopes – many unopened – letters, open books and magazines, small sheets of notepaper. The room looked as though it had been the unhappy recipient of a tickertape parade.

Cynthia airily waved her arms in an all-encompassing gesture, pointing out the obvious. "As you can see, I'm not overly tidy." She plomped herself down in a high-backed chair at the window end of the table and indicated that I was to sit beside her. "As you know, from our advertisement, I am an author. I write many, many things: books, articles, short stories, screenplays. I am *extremely* prolific."

Glancing at the scattered fruits of her labors, I believed her. I was impressed.

"Who is your publisher, Cynthia?" I asked. "Where have I read your stories?"

She was silent for a moment before saying, "To date those morons of the publishing world have not had the intelligence to recognize my ... I won't say *genius*," she said modestly, "but my style; my flair."

I felt less impressed and now understood the many large, unopened envelopes obviously containing rejected masterpieces.

"Your duties here will be many," she continued. "And they will be varied enough that I'm sure you won't get bored."

I was sure she was right and I could see that I might well enjoy being secretary to this eccentric, would-be author.

"You will take orders only from me, or from my . . . from John," she said. "In the morning, when she brings you your breakfast, you may let Sara know what you would like for lunch. She will bring it to you here, in the study, at midday. We all dine together in the dining room, every evening at seven-thirty. That's next to the sitting room we were in earlier. Any questions, child?"

I smarted. "Rebecca," I said.

"Any questions?" she repeated.

"Sara is the one who woke me this morning?" I asked. She nodded. "Er, how do I let her know what I want? She didn't seem to understand me too well when I asked her name."

Cynthia needlessly shuffled some papers into a pile. "Oh, don't worry, child. She may not say much at first, but she understands. She'll relay your wishes to cook."

"How many servants are there?" I asked. "You must need a lot with a big place like this."

"Come! You shall meet them. Perhaps we should have done that first."

Chapter Seven

Cynthia got up and stubbed out the remains of her cigarette in an ashtray that fought valiantly to keep its head above paper. She inserted a fresh cigarette into the holder and lit it. Then, together, we went out of the study and down the passageway, passing the wide entrance hall on our right.

"There is the dining room." Cynthia indicated a room on the left, which we passed. We moved on, passing another passage that crossed the main one at right-angles, and finally turned left into the kitchen.

It was a large room, just as I would have imagined a castle kitchen to be, with many shelves, alcoves, and closets. The floor was of huge stone slabs; the walls were rough plaster. It was generally ill-lit and gloomy and I wondered that anyone would work in such an atmosphere for any length of time. There was an old-fashioned laundry tub in one corner, complete with washboard and wringer, reminding me of the lack of electricity. Next to it was a voluminous sink, with dirty dishes piled on the draining board. I noticed a gas cooking range, though it was apparently little used. Most of the cooking was seemingly done at the fireplace. This was a huge, stone affair with an iron pot hanging over the fire from a pot-crane. Sara, the servant girl with the birthmark, was putting some small logs on the fire as we entered. She then swung a copper kettle over the flames. She turned when she heard us and, it seemed to me, cowered slightly at the sight of Cynthia. For her part, Cynthia seemed not to notice.

"Where's Frau Brūning?" my boss demanded.

As if in answer, a door at the end of the room opened and a plump, red-faced woman came in. She glanced at us briefly and then headed across to the sink where she began to noisily wash dishes as though we weren't there. She was dressed entirely in brown, her high-necked dress reaching to the floor and adding to the illusion of our having stepped back three centuries into the past. Her hair was tied up on top of her head in a severe bun. Mostly gray now I could see that it had once been a vivid red. She banged the dishes about with such vigor that I quite expected them to shatter.

"Frau Brūning, this is Rebecca, my new secretary."

The cook paused just briefly, with a quick glance over her shoulder that, despite its rapidity, obviously took in everything. She grunted "*Ja.*"

"I'm, er, very happy to meet you, Frau Brūning," I said, not quite certain how to address her.

"Where is Babula?" Cynthia looked about her, though it seemed certain no one else was in the great, gloomy kitchen.

The cook ignored her but Sara pointed hesitantly to the door through which she had entered.

"Ah! Follow me." Cynthia headed for the door.

I hurried after her, giving Sara a quick smile as I passed. I sensed, rather than saw, a flicker of friendship in her eyes in return.

The door led into a narrow, confining passageway that apparently ran between the outer wall of the castle and the rooms off the main corridor we had previously gone along. We passed an old, low, door set into the wall on the right and I surmised that it was the Tradesmen's Entrance Simon and I had first spotted.

Simon! I suddenly thought of him. How could I have let all thought of him slip from my mind so easily? Where was he? John had said that he left the previous night at about midnight. Yet I had seen Simon's jacket and shoes in his room two hours after that. Could my watch have been wrong? No, that was impossible or it would still have been wrong this morning. No, I didn't believe that Simon had left. But then, where was he? Had the Fletchers done something to him? But what? And why?

I was interrupted in my thoughts by Cynthia opening a door and stepping through into the sitting room. It was the same little door through which John had disappeared on two previous occasions. So the door led to the passage that, in turn, led to the kitchen.

I looked around the sitting room. At first I thought it was empty.

"*Memsahib?*"

I jumped. A figure materialized out of the gloom at the far end of the room. It was a man dressed all in white, which I reasoned should especially have made him stand out. Yet it seemed that one minute the room was empty and the next, he was there. He was not very tall – about my height, or even shorter – and was very dark skinned. His eyes seemed almost black; though bright and beady as they fastened on me. His eyelids hooded the eyes, like an eagle or – I thought with a shudder – a vulture! His black eyebrows almost met over his beak of a nose, to continue the comparison. His lips were small and thin, making his mouth appear as a slit. His clothes, with the Neru jacket, made me think him a Hindu. But what especially caught my attention was his headgear. He wore the traditional Indian turban, which made him appear taller than he actually was.

Something about the turban seemed familiar. Suddenly it hit me . . . it was the fisherman who was out in the boat last night! The man I had seen from Simon's window had looked as though he had his head bandaged. Now I realized what it was. I had seen this Indian, wearing his turban, down on the dock. But what had he been doing there at that hour, and so soon after the storm? Was he only fishing? I didn't think that this was the time to ask him.

"Rebecca," said Cynthia. "This is John's personal man, Babula."

I noticed that Cynthia hadn't called me "child" again, but was too fascinated by the Hindu to be overjoyed.

He placed his hands together, palm to palm, and bowed from the waist.

"*Memsahib*," was all he said. His voice was soft and low with a musical, almost hypnotic, lilt to it.

"Er, hi!" I replied self-consciously. I never seemed to know what to say at an introduction. "Nice being here."

He bowed again, moving silently backwards into the shadows, and I seemed to lose sight of him as Cynthia took my attention.

"At the end of each week you can make up a list of office supplies we may need. Babula will then pick them up when he goes across to the mainland. Now," she studied the stub in her cigarette-holder while the last of its ash cascaded, unnoticed, down her dress. "Let me see. You've met all the staff so I think we should get back to the study and do some work."

I was pleased to find John waiting for us in the study when we got back. He was sunk into one of the few easy chairs in the room, stroking a cat that crouched on his knees. At the sight of Cynthia the cat sprang up and moved swiftly to her side, rubbing itself against her ankles.

"Why, Sirdah!" cried Cynthia. "I wondered where you were. Come and meet Rebecca." She scooped up the cat and held him out towards me.

I tentatively reached out a hand to pet him but he spat at me and swung his claws. I hurriedly backed away.

"Naughty Sirdah," said Cynthia mildly, and put the cat down again. It padded back to John's chair and sat down beside it, eyeing me. Its black eyes reminded me of the Hindu, Babula, I had met just a short while before.

"Is he a Siamese?" I asked. "He looks , , , different, somehow."

"He's Burmese." John had been silent until now. He draped an arm over the chair and scratched the cat's ears. It ignored him. "Not too friendly, to strangers anyway. But he can be a very good watchdog, in his way." John got up and moved towards the door. "I just stopped by to mention a couple of things," he said.

He seemed somehow different, I thought. Sterner; slightly frightening, even. It made me feel a little like a schoolgirl caught doing something wrong. He looked at me and the warmth I had seen in his eyes before was not there.

"I would advise you to keep to the house, Rebecca," he said. "If you wish to go outside, while the weather is good, then keep to the front of the building. Don't wander off around the sides at all. I mention this for your own protection."

I thought of the wicked-toothed bear trap Simon and I had almost stumbled upon on our arrival. I had no wish to find similar signs of virulence.

"And within the castle," he continued, "I'm sure you will honor all locked doors. There are sections of the castle that have had to be closed off, since the building is incomplete . . . for the time being." He smiled, but there was no warmth in it. To Cynthia he said, "Why don't you go easy on Rebecca her first day? Give her a chance to settle in."

Cynthia, busy reloading her cigarette-holder, nodded and smiled at me over-sweetly. "Of course. I was thinking that myself." She waved airily at the paper-strewn table. "Why don't you just start-in trying to make some order out of this mess? We'll leave my dictating and such until tomorrow."

"Fine, Cynthia. Whatever you say," I said and watched her, and the cat, follow John out of the room.

I thought back to John's words: "I'm sure you will honor all locked doors . . ." I wondered what, exactly, he had meant by that. How could I do otherwise? If a door was locked, I had no key. Could he have known that I got my own door open the night before? I doubted it. But then, again, why had it been locked in the first place? Unless it was to keep me from checking on Simon. Simon! I hadn't forgotten him. I was determined to find out what had happened to him. And if that meant I had to get past locked doors, well . . . so be it!

Chapter Eight

Over the next few days I settled into the routine at Fletcher Castle. I became aware that John and Cynthia were very much alike in one way . . . they could both be very moody. I actually saw little of John; certainly not as much as I would have liked. When I did see him he was either very warm and friendly, or strangely distant and rather frightening. Cynthia's mood changed with the wind. Her memory was not the best either. In good humor she would send me on an errand to the kitchen but when I returned, a short time later, I would find her in a towering rage demanding to know where I had been. Luckily I am a very patient person and do not easily get upset, so I was able to pacify her at times like those.

I regretted I had little time to search, in any way extensively, for Simon. I was no longer locked in my room at night, which led me to believe, all the more strongly, that the reason for that first night's confinement was connected with Simon's disappearance. What little exploration of the castle I was able to carry out produced nothing. I investigated all the many rooms on the second floor, in the west half of the castle, and a number in the east. Most of the rooms were bare and empty; others contained only a few sticks of furniture. All were laden with dust, showing no sign of having been disturbed in a long time. I encountered locked doors, terminating the corridors at their ends in both directions. I decided that if I were to make any headway at all I would need to get past these barriers.

One morning, after an hour or so of dictating extremely rude letters to publishers who had rejected her, Cynthia asked me to go to the castle library to get a particular book she needed. She was contemplating writing a history of the lake, and of Fletcher Island in particular. As a matter of fact I had given her the idea myself by dropping a few hints. It seemed to be a subject she might do very well and one that might stand a chance of actually getting published.

"It's a thick one," she said, referring to the book she needed. "With a blue, or green, cover. Should be somewhere in that section to the left of the door as you go in. The title is something like *Turn of the Century on Winnepesaukee*. I don't know who the author was."

I nodded and left the study. The library was the other side of the main entrance hall, opposite the dining room. I had been there two or three times before but never alone. It was quite an impressive room, with bookcases floor to ceiling on every wall. The window, which looked out over the roof of the boathouse, down at the lake's edge, was strangely small for a library. I would have thought it necessary to have good light in the room, especially since some of the books were ancient, leather-bound tomes with worn lettering at the spine.

There was a refectory table in the center of the room, though considerably smaller than the one in the study. A small gesso table stood gleaming under the window and there were a half-dozen high-backed, cane-seated chairs scattered about the room.

I turned to the section of books on my left. Someone, at some time, had gone to a lot of trouble putting the books into some semblance of order. In the section I studied they were all travel and history books. They dealt with every country imaginable. Among the ones on New England, I quickly spotted one titled *Around the Turn of the Century, About Lake Winnepesaukee*. It had a red cover. I took the book over to the gesso table by the window and opened it.

It had been published in 1908 in Boston, and contained a brief passage on how the lake got its name. I had wondered ever since arriving there and was intrigued to find that the Native American name meant "The Smile of the Great Spirit." It was tied-in with a delightful legend concerning a young chief named Adiwando and his love for Mineola, daughter of the chief of a hostile tribe. Apparently after much ill will and misunderstanding between father and prospective son-in-law, Adiwando and Mineola eloped. The irate father was finally pacified when he saw the sun come out from behind a cloud and shine down on the sparkling waters around their departing canoe. "It is a good omen," he said. "Hereafter these waters shall be known as "The Smile of the Great Spirit. *(Winnepesaukee)*". It was a sweet story that I liked . . . whether or not it was true!

I had picked up the book and started to leave the library when I noticed a section of bookcase in the far corner of the room, away from the window. Unlike the rest of the cases, this section was glass-fronted and – as I discovered when I tried to open it – locked. I peered through the glass at the titles but could make out little. All of the books were bound in black leather.

"Missss Rebecca!"

I nearly jumped out of my skin. I dropped the book I was holding and spun around. There stood Babula, hands together, bowing to me. The way he had drawn out the esses of "Miss" had made me think of a snake. His bright, beady eyes added to the thought.

"Goodness! You startled me!" I said, retrieving the book I'd dropped.

He bowed again.

"I didn't hear you come in." I was a little angry. There was surely no need for him to go sneaking about, frightening people like that. "Did you have to be so – so quiet?"

He bowed deeply yet again and moved towards the door. In a moment he was gone.

I returned to the study feeling very angry and complained to Cynthia. She shrugged her shoulders.

"Babula is like that," was all she said, then added: "You will have to get used to him."

To put the nasty little man out of my mind I started questioning Cynthia about Fletcher Island. "Who was the first Fletcher here? Why did he build the castle?"

She seemed happy to relax and chat for a while.

"That was Henry Fletcher, John's grandfather. But really, to understand you have to go back to the beginning."

"The beginning?"

"Well, just about, yes. The name Fletcher, you know, means a man who makes arrows. I think it's actually connected more specifically with the feathers on an arrow; the 'flights' they're called. But anyway . . ."

"Then that's where your coat-of-arms comes from," I said.

"The crest? Yes, with the arm and the fist full of arrows. Right. Anyway, way back in the sixteenth century – I think it was – in England, one of John's ancestors was knighted because of his prowess at making arrows. That was Sir Gilbert Fletcher. And Sir Gilbert had a castle built."

"Where did he get the money?" I wondered aloud. "It was one thing to make arrows well enough to get knighted, but finding the money to build a castle, even in those days . . ."

"Perhaps he just sold a lot of arrows," said Cynthia, a two-inch length of ash detaching itself from her cigarette and dusting her bosom. "Anyway, he built a castle and lived a life of leisure for many, many years until he was killed in an accident."

"What sort of accident?"

"I think one of his serfs chopped off his head with a scythe. But to get back to the present. The Fletcher family seemed to have quite enough money to live well, right down to John's grandfather's time. He – Henry Fletcher – came to America from England and decided to build his own castle, right here on Fletcher Island. Unfortunately it cost far more than he expected and he ran out of money before he could complete it."

"What a shame," I said. "He must really have been caught up in the old family history to even think of doing something like that. He must have been tremendously disappointed that he couldn't finish it."

"Yes, he was," said Cynthia drily. "He threw himself off the newly completed East Tower."

"Oh!"

"John's father, William, tried to find the money to finish the job, as John himself has done, but no luck so far," she ended.

"Do you think it ever will get finished?" I asked. "It doesn't look as though there's *too* much more to be done."

"There's enough. As a matter of fact John does have certain . . . certain ideas." She suddenly stood up. "I'm bored. I think I'm going to my room to take a nap. Why don't you do the same? We'll leave all this dusty old history and start fresh tomorrow."

I was surprised but since it was seldom she gave me time off I didn't argue. I didn't particularly want to take a nap but I did think I'd wander around a bit. As Cynthia headed for her room, I went through the sitting room to the passage that led to the kitchen. I intended to go and talk to Frau Brüning, the cook. I had seen little of her in the few days I had been at the castle, and it would be nice to talk to someone other than the Fletchers, for a change.

The passageway was narrow and, from the dust I felt on the moldings running along the walls, was seldom cleaned. Since Sara was the only person I had ever seen doing any sort of house cleaning, I was not surprised there was so much dust throughout the castle. The place was much too big to be kept clean by one small girl.

As I came level with the old Tradesmen's Door, I paused. Something had been gnawing at the back of my mind for some time. It was Simon's boat. Was it still out at the little dock, were we had landed?

If it was, then obviously Simon was still at the castle. I tried the handle of the old door. It was locked but a rusty key was sticking out of the lock. I tried to turn it. Stiff with rust, and age, it would not move at first. But I persisted. Suddenly, with a grinding, it turned and the bolt inside moved back. Putting my shoulder to it, I got the warped old door to creak open just enough to allow me to slip through. I stood outside and breathed deeply. The fresh air felt good.

In case anyone should pass along the passageway, I pushed the door closed again and prayed that no one would lock it. Then I set off down the path, through the trees.

Chapter Nine

It didn't take long to reach the landing stage where Simon and I had arrived, it seemed so long ago. I felt almost disappointed when I came in sight of it and found the dock deserted. There was no boat tied there. I felt torn in two. I wanted Simon to be well and safe yet I knew, instinctively, that he was not. Did the fact that his boat was not there mean that he had truly left? Or did it simply mean that the Fletchers were smart enough to have hidden it?

The Fletchers? . . . John! What was I implying about John? There were times, certainly, when I could imagine all sorts of horrible things connected to him. Yet there were also times . . . times when he looked at me in a certain way, with those hypnotic gray eyes of his. When I could in no way imagine him capable of hurting even a fly.

Suddenly my attention was caught by something down in the murky water, at the far end of the dock. It was something lying down at the bottom of the lake. I couldn't make out what it was; just something large but about the size of a . . . small rowing boat . . . and blue! Simon's dinghy had been blue! I was about to start forward to investigate when a noise, in the woods behind me, stopped me. I could feel a pair of eyes looking at me. I turned slowly, expecting to see the mysterious Babula.

Instead I was surprised, and a little disconcerted, to see the cat Sirdah. The cat was standing in the middle of the path, as still as a statue, its bright eyes fastened on me. I didn't know whether or not it was from the way the light caught them, but those eyes seemed to glow red, like burning coals, boring into me. I felt suddenly as though I ought to apologize; to explain my being where I was. I shook myself and laughed out loud at the idea. The sound seemed to startle the cat. It turned, moving slowly, and disappeared into the underbrush.

Without checking to see what it was down in the water – some other day, I thought – I hurried back up the trail towards the castle. Moving uphill took longer than coming down, I found, and I was panting when I finally arrived at the old door. It was still closed, as I had left it. It was as I again forced it open and squeezed inside that a thought struck me. How had the cat got out? This door was closed. Surely Sirdah hadn't wandered all around the outside of the castle, with those ugly bear traps lying about.

I felt much better once inside the castle again. My encounter with the strange cat had unnerved me more than I had at first thought. I kicked myself for rushing back without at least checking on the shape I thought I had spotted down below the surface of the lake. *Could* it be Simon's boat? Now I would have to get out again, sometime, to make certain.

I made my way to the kitchen and was pleased to see Sara there, peeling potatoes. She looked up as I entered and smiled her crooked smile.

"Hello, Sara," I said. "I thought I'd do a little socializing. Where's Frau Brüning?"

Sara nodded in the direction of the pantry in the corner. As I looked that way the large, brown-clad figure of the cook emerged, a carton of milk in her hand. Her knitted brow and pouting expression made me wonder whether she would be such a refreshing change from our employer after all.

"Hello, Frau Brüning," I said. "I thought I'd stop by and chat for a while, if I may? If you're not too busy? I'd really like to get to know you, since we both work in such a – er – restricted place."

She banged the milk down on the table and, taking up a teapot, headed for the big copper kettle singing over the fire.

"Hm. *Ja!* Restricted is right." She poured a little of the boiling liquid into the teapot, swirled it around, then crossed to the sink and tipped it out. "I don't know that I have time for idle chatter," she said. She started ladling loose tea into the pot. "You want, maybe, cup of tea?"

I nodded. "Yes, I'd love one." I thought that despite her stern exterior, Frau Brüning might be a good friend to have. Something in her eyes told me that much of her rigid severity was a façade for dominance in the kitchen. It was obvious she held Sara in fear, if not her employers also. I watched the tea-making ritual continue.

"Always – *always* – take the pot to the kettle," she said sternly, as though lecturing a domestic science class. She marched across to the steaming kettle and poured boiling water onto the tea. "Now it will steep for precisely three minutes."

She put the lid on the teapot and covered it with a heavy tea cozy. Sara watched all this, her eyes wide with wonder. She must have witnessed the ceremony at least once a day for as long as she had been at the castle, but it obviously never lost its fascination.

"Sit down. Sit down, *fräulein*, out of the way. I don't want you under my feet!"

I smiled and took a seat at the kitchen table. "Won't you call me Rebecca?" I asked. "Tell me, Frau Brūning, how long have you been at Fletcher Castle?"

Going noisily about her duties, the granite-faced martinet slowly opened up.

"How long? Hah! How long has this monstrosity been here? *Nein.* I have been here thirty-eight years."

"As long as that? Don't you ever get lonely here?"

"Hmm." She shrugged her shoulders. "What is 'lonely'?" She removed the tea cozy and poured three cups of tea, pushing one across to Sara who grabbed it up and scampered across to sit on a stool by the fire.

I learned that the cook had come to Fletcher Castle with her husband, Otto, straight from Germany, at the outbreak of the Second World War. Her husband had died of cancer ten years ago, she said, and she was now quite content to spend the rest of her days running the Fletchers' kitchen.

"You must have known Mr. Fletcher's father, then," I said.

"Mr. William?" She looked at me sharply. For a moment I thought she had turned pale, all the color draining from that full, strong face. But

I must have been mistaken for a moment later I saw that she was as ruddy as ever, though it almost seemed there was a trace of fear in her eyes.

"Mr. William is . . . all right, *Ja*? He is all right?"

"*Is?* You mean he's still alive?"

"What?" The cook seemed to suddenly realize what she had said. "*Nein!* No! No. I live in the past a lot, you understand? No, Mr. William is . . . no longer with us."

She pushed her cup of tea to one side, came to her feet, and started chopping vegetables, making – it seemed to me – a great deal of unnecessary noise. Sara came to her feet, looking frightened, and ran around trying to anticipate the cook's wishes.

"What did you mean, Mr. William Fletcher is 'all right'?"

It was a while before Frau Brūning answered. When she did she was quite calm.

"Just that, fräulein Rebecca. He was all right. He was good man to work for. He was good employer."

"Oh, I see." I thought to change the subject. "This lake is really beautiful. I wish I were a photographer; I'd love to take some pictures of it."

"You do not paint?"

"I've done a little watercolor. I'm not very good, though. Still, that is an idea. Perhaps I'll do one of the lake. I do have my paints with me."

"That would be nice."

I gave it some thought. "From the top of the castle would give the best view, I guess. Is it safe to go up on the battlements, do you know?"

"You would have to ask Mr. John."

"Yes, of course." I had an idea. "Oh! What about the tower? I bet the view from the top of the tower is fantastic."

The knife she had been using crashed down against the table.

"*Nein! Nein.* You do not go near the East Tower. *Nein!* Mr. John he would never allow it. No, you must paint from . . . from somewhere else. Now I have work to do. I cannot be talking all day. Away with you now!"

I was shooed unceremoniously out of the kitchen. Somewhat shaken by the mercurial temperament of the cook – which I thought almost rivaled Cynthia's – I headed for the main hall, deciding to go down to the big dock and look around the boathouse. I felt the need for a breath of air.

As I turned the corner and came into view of the foot of the grand staircase, I encountered Babula who had apparently just come down from the upper floors. He bowed deeply to me, as he always did, and glided silently away and around the corner of the corridor, the way I had just come. So far as I knew, his room was in the servants' quarters, in the north corner of the castle. The Fletchers' suite was in the east corner, but it was on the ground floor so he couldn't have been coming from there. There was just no reason that I could think of for Babula to have been coming down the main staircase.

I shrugged my shoulders but, instead of going outside the house, I turned and started to climb the stairs to my room. Perhaps I should take a nap before dinner after all? I had encountered too many problems, temperaments, illusions, for one day. An appearing and disappearing Hindu, an almost human cat, an employer *and* a cook who changed moods at the drop of a hat, the ever-present question of Simon's whereabouts. All this was too much for me, I decided. I thankfully opened the door to my room and went in.

I don't know what it was that made me feel uneasy, but something did. I stood in the center of the room looking about me almost as though I expected someone, or something, to jump out at me. Nothing, and no one, did. I walked over to the window and looked out. Over the treetops, I could see the lake. I felt cheered by the sight of it. Away in the distance I could make out the shore of the mainland, with mountains rising behind the omnipresent evergreens. It seemed so far away.

I turned to the bachelor chest and my eye was caught by a piece of blue material sticking out from one of the drawers. It was a pale blue half-slip of mine, which had got caught as someone had closed the drawer in a hurry. I say "someone" because I know that I hadn't left it like that. As I checked and saw the way various articles of my clothing had been folded, I knew quite definitely that someone had been there. Someone had been through all my belongings! But why? What were they looking for? What did they think I had to hide?

Chapter Ten

"In the old days there were three boathouses and we had a continuous stream of people going backwards and forwards to the mainland. We had parties here that were talked about for months afterwards. We had costume balls and medieval-style banquets in the Great Hall."

John's face glowed as he sat, swinging his legs, on the stone wall at the foot of the front lawn above the docks. I sat beside him, trying to imagine the great gloomy castle behind us full of lights and fun and people. It wasn't easy, though John's description helped.

"How old were you then, John?" I asked. His gray eyes connected with mine and I felt a thrill run through me. I looked away again before I should blush.

"I was only a child," he said. "But I've never forgotten those days. I've made a vow to bring them back."

His voice was suddenly grim and I looked up to see his brow furrowed and his face dark; a strange light replacing the dreaminess I had seen in his eyes just a moment before. One moment this tall, attractive man would charm me, drawing me strongly to him, but the next he would frighten me. My, but these Fletchers were changeable, I thought! As if in response to my feelings John's face suddenly turned bright again. He dropped down from the wall and, taking me firmly about the waist, swung me down beside him.

"Come on, Rebecca," he said. "Let's go for a walk."

It was Sunday and, as he had done for my last three days off, John was giving me "a break from Cynthia", as he put it. I must admit I had come to look forward to these times alone with John. We would usually spend some of it just sitting by the docks. One time I had even tried dabbling my feet in the water, but it was too late in the year and my feet almost froze! We would go exploring along the front, south-east shore of the island. Never did we go to the sides or the back of the castle.

"How is Cynthia this morning?" I asked.

"Why do you ask?"

"Oh, I don't know," I said. "It's just that lately she's been making me feel like a husband-stealer."

"What do you mean by that?"

I was surprised at the way he snapped out the question and I gasped with pain when he suddenly grabbed my wrist, tightly.

"Oh, John! Please. You're hurting me."

"I'm sorry." He let go of my wrist but continued to look intently at me. "I didn't mean to hurt you. But . . . what did you mean by what you said?"

I rubbed my wrist. "Don't get so excited," I said. "I just meant that lately Cynthia has been behaving very – well – jealously. Always for a day or so after we have been out here like this. It's almost as though she were your wife, not your sister. That's all I meant."

"Oh." He sounded relieved. "I'm sorry, Rebecca. I didn't mean to grab you so tightly. I'll speak to Cynthia. She should know better. It's just that we've been alone here for so long that I guess she does feel a little jealous. But that's ridiculous. I'll tell her to cut it out."

"I guess it's not ridiculous," I said, as we walked on. "Actually, I can well understand it." I looked at him archly. "You should be flattered."

He threw back his head and laughed. I loved it when he was happy. He took my hand and we plunged ahead between the closely growing trees. It seemed a perfectly natural action, for him to take my hand like that, but the feel of my hand in his was almost more than I could bear. I was nearly afraid to grip in case he thought I gripped too hard and was being forward. Yet at the same time, if I didn't grip at all he might think I was discouraging him . . . which I certainly did not want to do. I was not in a quandary for long, however, for as we entered a clearing he let go of my hand and went over to a huge rock, thrusting up five or six feet out of the ground.

"Here!" he said. "Let me help you up on to the top of this. There's something I want you to see."

We scrambled up to stand breathlessly, side by side, on the flat top of the boulder.

"Look! There, at the castle." He pointed.

His voice was almost in awe and I saw why. From that vantage point we could see, towering up behind the trees, the bold, impressive, east corner of the castle. The great tower was directly in front of us and, as I looked at it, I could recognize the power and determination in the building. It was like something out of a history book suddenly come to life. When inside the castle you tended to forget the overall effect of the outside. For several minutes we stood there in silence.

"You must be very proud," I said finally, in a hushed voice.

"I am," he replied quietly.

"I would love to paint a picture of it. Perhaps next Sunday I might bring my paints out here?"

He beamed. "Why, that's a splendid idea, Rebecca."

He put his arm lightly about my waist, to steady me. As he looked into my eyes, so close, I felt my heart thumping. Surely he must hear it, I thought; it's so loud? His eyes held mine. They seemed so large; so inviting. Like – what was the expression? – like "limpid pools". They seemed to grow bigger. No, he was closer. His face drew closer to mine. Time seemed to stand still. A faint, musky smell touched my nostrils. It must have been his aftershave. It had a heady effect on me. My eyelids fluttered, and closed.

"What do *you* want?"

John's sharp, angry shout brought me back to reality with a bang. I almost fell from the rock. In fact I would have done if John had not kept a tight hold on me. I followed the direction of his angry gaze and saw Babula kowtowing obsequiously at the edge of the clearing.

"Don't just stand there, you – you – imbecile!"

I had never seen John so angry. Yet, thinking back to the moment before, I tended to share his anger.

"Your pardon, Esteemed One." Babula bowed even lower. "It was not my intention to give you anger. Forgive this unworthy servant."

"Just get the devil on with what you have to say," snorted John. "Here, Rebecca. Let me help you down."

We clambered down, John catching me as I almost tripped at the bottom. He held me just a fraction longer than was actually necessary before turning again to the Hindu.

"Well?"

"Your pardon, sir. It was the desire of your esteemed . . . of the *Memsahib* Fletcher that I pursue you and advise you of the need of your presence."

"What's wrong?"

"It is, indeed, the matter to which you had previously instructed me to give my humble attention, *Sahib*. I must beg of you to come at once."

John turned to me and put his hands on my shoulders.

"I'm sorry, Rebecca," he said softly. "I have to leave you. Something needs my attention back at the castle. I'm so sorry."

He kissed me lightly on the forehead and, together with Babula, hurried off into the trees. For the longest time I stood where I was, feeling his lips on my forehead. If Babula had not made his untimely appearance, would I have felt those lips on mine? I had disliked the sneaky Hindu before; now I almost hated him! I smiled at the line my thoughts were taking.

At a leisurely pace, I walked back through the trees towards the dock. It was still early afternoon and, although large clouds were gathering, I didn't feel like going back into the castle until I had to. I looked about me as I walked. Over the trees I could see the top of the

East Tower. With no particular purpose in mind, I made my way towards it.

The closer I got, the larger loomed the tower, until finally I stood at its foot straining my neck to look up. There was to be a sister great round tower at the other end of the castle front, but that had still to be built. The smaller towers at the back of the castle were square ones. The East Tower, then, dominated the whole structure, but giving the castle a slightly lopsided appearance. It – like the rest of the castle – was built of huge slabs of native granite. The lower section was plain but from about a third of the way up the surface was broken by an occasional window. These openings were tall and narrow. They were not as narrow as arrow slits but they gave the same impression. At the top floor of the tower there was a very large window that overlooked the lake to the east. It resembled a modern picture window, and as such seemed incongruous set, as it was, in the solid stone of the tower wall. The top of the tower itself was castellated, like the battlements of the main building.

I walked slowly around the foot of the tower, to the right, away from the front of the castle. There were many rough rocks and scrubby bushes that hindered me, but I slowly worked my way back until I could see where the tower joined the side of the castle. There, at the join, was a small door looking much like the Tradesmen's Entrance at the rear of the castle. I was about to approach it when something caught my eye. I picked up a long, dead branch and used it to reach forward and move a hanging branch out of the way. I gasped. There on the ground, partially hidden, was another of the vicious, steel-jawed, bear traps. It was right where anyone might step if they were going to enter the tower . . . or try to leave it. I decided I must ask John about them.

I returned the way I had come, back around the tower to the front. There were no other doors. As I was about to clamber over the last of the rocks, I halted. There in front of me, reminding me somehow of a rattlesnake, was Sirdah the cat. As at the previous time when he had found me at the old dock, he sat absolutely still with his strange redish eyes fixed on me. For a moment I couldn't help comparing the hypnotic fascination of those eyes with John's.

"I – I'm just looking around," I stammered. Then I mentally kicked myself. What was I doing apologizing to a cat? "I just went around the tower and back," I found myself continuing. "I'm going into the house now."

This was crazy! I didn't have to account for myself to Sirdah. Not only that, but I had no intention of going back into the castle for a while. Or had I? The cat stood up. It gave me one last, lingering look, and then padded away. I watched it disappear under a bush. I found myself moving, as though in a dream, towards the front entrance to the castle.

Once inside I shook myself. I was letting both my nerves and my imagination run away with themselves. Perhaps I'd been intending to come inside anyway, I told myself. After all, it was beginning to get very cold and windy outside. Perhaps it was all something to do with the unconscious mind using the cat as a means of making its wishes known to the conscious mind . . . or something? I never had been much good at psychology. Anyway, now that I was in, I decided I should do something constructive. I headed for the library. I hadn't been there for about a week and, from the look of it, neither had anyone else. There was a fine film of dust visible on the tops of both the refectory table and the gesso table. Well, there was something I could do, I thought. I could dust. It would be a change for me plus a help for Sara. I went along to the kitchen, got Sara to understand what I wanted, and returned to the library armed with a feather duster, a spray can of *Pledge*, and some rags. For half an hour I worked happily, dusting and polishing.

Eventually I worked my way around to that section of the shelves with the glass doors. I peered in at the black-bound volumes. The light from the window was a little brighter than the last time I had studied the books; the time I was interrupted by Babula. Nervously I looked around, half expecting to see the bowing figure in white standing watching me. But I was alone. I turned back to the books.

Lemegaton, Heptameron, Sacred Magic of Abra-Melin the Mage, Grimoire of Honorius, Almadel, Pansophy of Rudolph the Magus, The Greater Key of Solomon the King. What strange titles! Instinctively I tried the glass-paneled doors. They were locked, yet they gave a little. I saw that the retaining hook on the left side door was not properly in place. I gently tapped and, sure enough, the hook slipped completely out of its eye. Although the lock was closed, the two doors were then free to swing out and the lock to separate. Nervously I reached in and removed one of the books.

It was a thick, heavy tome and I opened it randomly somewhere near the middle. The book was obviously very old and the edges of the pages were brown and brittle, almost as though they had been singed. There were strange figures, or diagrams, on the pages and below them words, or perhaps names, followed by descriptions. *MURMUR*, I read. *A military Duke and Earl, who rideth upon a Griffin. His crown pronounceth his status, and his voice be ever harsh. Upon evocation he will be attended upon by two heralds. Murmur teacheth all philosophies and causeth souls long dead to appear before the Circle.*

A little lower was another, equally mystifying, description: *PAIMON: Directly under the Supreme One. Those who knoweth his Seal and calleth upon him in accordance with the ritual, gain any honor from him. He confereth the power to dominate all men and will produce useful familiar spirits to serve the Magus.*

Intrigued, I turned a couple of pages. It made no sense to me. Suddenly a name caught my eye; a name I knew only too well: *SIRDAH: A powerful warrior who may be conjured with the given sigil. A trusted servant, once commanded Sirdah provideth all information sought, will guard and protect the Magus, and will report efficiently all information requested. Sirdah may assume any shape but hath a preference for that of a cat.*

I closed the book with a bang. *May assume any shape but hath a preference for that of a cat!* What did this mean? Surely not what I thought. Sirdah – the Fletchers' Sirdah – was a little unusual, yes, but . . . but what? Was he some sort of demon in animal form? But that was ridiculous . . . wasn't it? And anyway, how would he have got here? Who would have "conjured" him? Somehow I couldn't see Cynthia as a magician. I smiled at the thought and felt a little better. But then I thought of Babula.

Another thought struck me and, almost panicking, I opened the book again. Frantically turning the pages, I found the Bs. I ran a shaking finger down the page. No; there was no Babula listed. Again I smiled to myself. At least *he* wasn't a demon! I carefully replaced the book and closed the two doors, bringing them together so that the lock slid into place. Picking up my dusting implements, I left the library and headed for my room. I would return the duster later. Right now I needed to think.

By the time I reached my room and sank down, flat on my back on the bed, I had made some sense out of the near panic brought on by my over-zealous imagination. I soberly told myself that I was putting the cart before the horse. Cynthia, or John, had come across the name Sirdah in that old book of nonsense and had decided to give it to their cat. Simple! At least I hoped it was. Yet somehow, no matter how much I tried to put it out of my mind, my thoughts kept returning to that entry in the book; kept picking it over. Sirdah did seem to have a mind of his own. He did seem to appear and disappear as though checking on my movements. And John had said that, although a cat, "Sirdah could be a very good watchdog".

I got up, went into the bathroom, and washed my face with cold water. It felt good. And it seemed to help clear my head of these wild fancies. I looked at my watch and decided I should do something other than take a nap before dinner. It would seem a sin to just waste away my spare time. I determined to do a little more exploring inside the castle.

Chapter Eleven

I took the broken-handled candle snuffer I had used to unlock my own door that first night – so long ago now, it seemed – and, just in case I met someone, tucked it under my sweater. I set off down a corridor at the rear of the castle. However there was a locked door at the end of it and this was my first obstacle.

It seemed that all of the locks in the castle were suitably medieval in design. They were big, bulky, iron boxes with huge keyholes, stoutly fastened to the solid oak beams of the doors. On these locked doors, unfortunately, all the keyholes were empty. I inserted the curved end of the candle snuffer and started wriggling it about, first one way and then the other. After five minutes I gave up. After the ease with which it had opened my own door, I felt very disappointed. What to do now? Then I suddenly remembered the one big lock in which I had seen a key: the Tradesmen's Door. I wondered if there was any chance that old key might fit some of the other locks? It was worth a try.

I went back to my room, gathered up my dusting implements, and went down to return them to the kitchen. No one was there; in fact the whole castle seemed deserted. Were they all taking naps? I didn't wait to find out but made my way back to the staircase by way of the back passage and the door through the sitting room. As I passed the old door in the outer wall, I pulled the rusty key from its lock and stuck it down the top of my jeans.

I half expected to find John or Cynthia, or even Babula, in the sitting room but, like the kitchen, it was empty. Gratefully I scurried up the stairs and along the passage to my room. I took a couple of minutes to catch my breath and wait for my heart to stop thumping, then I went out of the room again and back down the corridor to the locked door. I put the old key into the lock and turned it.

Surprisingly it clicked open as though it were well-oiled and frequently used. I removed the key, sticking it back in my jeans, and went through the door carefully closing it behind me. I was faced with a further dusty short section of corridor leading into another cross-passageway. I could go either to the left or the right. I would need to go right to get to the West Tower, I knew, but I took the time to go left first.

I found two more empty rooms and then, as I turned back, I saw another door. I opened it and peered in. I gasped and drew back. It was the entrance to the Minstrel Gallery, high up on the wall of the Great Banquet Hall. John had once taken me into the hall, at the ground level, to show me the beautiful stained glass windows set high in the outer walls. Now I could see those windows, their upper points on a level with where I stood. The gallery itself seemed small and had a frightening low parapet. If I leaned over it I knew I would see the big oak dining table on the stone floor below. I had no desire to risk tumbling down on it. Carefully I backed out and closed the door.

I headed across, past the corridor that had led me to this end of the castle, along and around the far corner to the stone steps leading up into the west square tower. The west and north square towers were no more than shells for these outer stairways, I realized, unlike the mighty east and unfinished south round towers which seemed to contain rooms, though whether for storage or habitation I didn't know.

I emerged on the third floor and started down a corridor that must have run immediately above the one on the floor below. Again I found empty rooms, until the last door before the locked passageway door of this upper floor. This last door I opened expecting to see just another dusty, empty bedroom. Instead, I found a cornucopia of thought-provoking articles. The room was full of boxes, suitcases, clothing, handbags, shoes, hats, coats; a veritable thrift-shop supply house, it seemed. There was no particular order, with clothing thrown over suitcases and boxes on top of coats. Most of the clothing was old, giving me the impression that it had been there for a long time. But there were also some more recent additions, I found.

I had just concluded that this was where John and Cynthia dumped their cast-offs, when I spotted a pair of cut-off jeans shorts . . . the sort of thing that I might wear in the summer. And about my size too, I thought. But they were decidedly not the kind of thing worn by Cynthia. I pulled away a box in the corner where the shorts were, and found a lot more similar items of clothing. It was all for a girl of about my size, though perhaps a little fuller in the bosom. There was one very beautiful, pale yellow blouse trimmed with white lace. It had a name embroidered on the pocket: *Julie*. The name seemed to ring a far-distant bell, but I couldn't place it.

Whose clothes were these? And why were they stored here, behind locked doors? They were all good, little-worn items. Why were they dumped here, in such a haphazard manner? I was about to leave the room and return to my own when something caught my eye. Something red – a bright, nylon-silky material – was half-covered by a fallen suitcase. I moved the case and pulled out the object. It was a windbreaker . . . and I would have sworn it was Simon's.

Back in my room I stood, for the longest time, staring out of the window. Over the few brief weeks I had been at Fletcher Castle I had slowly allowed my curiosity to dim about Simon's disappearance. Now – abruptly; rudely – I had been brought back to reality. If that *was* Simon's windbreaker in the room above, then there was proof that Simon had never left the island. If he was alive – and I shuddered to think of the alternative – then he must surely be somewhere in the castle. But where? And why was he being held here? I had to renew my search, with vigor. No more taking things easy! After all, I reminded myself, I was the one responsible for Simon coming to Fletcher Island in the first place.

The water of the lake was very rough; covered with whitecaps whipped up by the wind. I was about to turn away from the grim grayness of the water when I realized what I had been watching while thinking of my discovery. There was a boat bouncing about, out there on the rough water. I realized that I had been watching it without being conscious of doing so; seeing it come closer and closer to the island. Who could it be? Surely no one would attempt to come to Fletcher in weather like this? Though perhaps they had been out in the center of the lake when the weather changed for the worst. Perhaps they were just aiming at the island in search of security. Some security, I thought bitterly!

Something in the boat glinted. As far away from me as it was, I realized that the orange-clad figure steering the vessel was also trying to keep a pair of binoculars trained on the castle. Although the boat seemed powerful, he must have had his hands full just getting through the rough water without also scanning the battlements. As the boat disappeared from view behind the trees, I turned from the window and went into the bathroom to prepare for dinner.

I was surprised when, almost an hour later, as I was about to go downstairs, Sara tapped on my door and came in carrying a tray.

"Sara! What's this? Why the tray?"

She put it down on top of the bachelor chest and, studying me, lifted the cover of the tureen and grunted.

"Dinner?" I asked.

She nodded enthusiastically.

"But – but I always go down to the dining room for dinner, to join Mr. and Mrs. Fletcher. In fact, I was just about to go down now."

She vigorously shook her head from side to side and pointed to the tray.

"Who said I had to eat up here?" I demanded. "Mr. Fletcher?"

Again she nodded. I began to feel angry.

"That's ridiculous! I'm not going to eat my dinner up here."

Panic covered Sara's face and she backed away from me.

"I'm sorry, Sara. It's not your fault. I shouldn't snap at you. Okay, off you go. And thank you."

Obviously relieved, the slight figure ran from the room. But I was not mollified. Why should John suddenly want me to eat in my room? Why, without warning, was I being told – in effect – not to go downstairs? I determined to find out. I threw a cardigan around my shoulders and headed for the stairs.

As I reached the bottom of the staircase I heard voices coming from the sitting room. Unless I was mistaken there were two male voices. One I recognized as John's. I moved across the hallway, opened the sitting room door, and went in. John, who was facing me with his back to the fireplace, looked up in obvious surprise.

"Rebecca! I thought I . . . Oh, I'm glad you came down after all."

Standing facing him, with his back to me, was a man in an orange slicker. The driver of the boat I had seen from my window.

He turned around as John addressed me. He was of medium height, with black hair, and brown eyes that swept over me with obvious approval. I ignored the look and decided that I did not care for his thin lips and sharp features. He was not much older than me. His bulky sweater, under the slicker, and his heavy corduroy pants, did not conceal his slim but wiry frame. He smiled and, despite my momentary dislike, I found his smile warm and friendly.

"Hi!" he said. His voice matched his smile.

"Er, Rebecca, this is Peter . . ."

"Southwood." He kept his dancing eyes on my face.

"Peter Southwood. Yes." John folded his arms, as he did when generally displeased. "Mr. Southwood is here, so he says, to talk business with Cynthia."

I had to smile back at Peter Southwood. His smile was infectious.

"I'm Rebecca Valentine," I said, and put out my hand. "Miss Fletcher's secretary."

"*Very* pleased to meet you, Ms. Valentine."

He took my hand in both of his and held it longer than necessary. It was not until I caught sight of John's dark frown that I pulled away. Just then Cynthia sailed into the room carrying a small tray on which rested three wine glasses and a decanter. She seemed surprised to see me but recovered quickly.

"Ah, Rebecca," she gushed. "Isn't it exciting? Mr. Southwood's company wants to make a movie of one of my books!"

Chapter Twelve

The weather took a decided turn for the worse. It seemed it was going to be an early winter. Even if Peter Southwood had wanted to leave he would not have been able to, the lake had become far too rough. Yet he showed no desire to complete his business in any kind of hurry. He quite belied the impression I held of Hollywood movie moguls. Admittedly, though, he had said that he was actually based in New York.

I still had difficulty accepting the fact that one of Cynthia's stories had found favor with a movie company. So, I knew, had John. Yet here was Peter Southwood to prove it. He claimed that one of the publishers to whom Cynthia had first sent her book, was a personal friend of his boss. Although the publisher couldn't use it, said Peter, he thought the story would make a good movie and so he passed on the word. The book was a rambling story of life in a Vermont village. Not at all the sort of thing to set the screen afire, I thought. But then, what did I know about box-office appeal? Apparently Peter, and his company, thought otherwise.

Peter suggested that Cynthia put the novel into screenplay form, and he worked with her on it. I did most of the typing, of course. I would have liked to have asked Peter more about the movie industry, but

Cynthia was ever present and John put in frequent appearances, so I couldn't help noticing that I was never allowed to be alone with Peter.

It was late one evening, two days after Peter's arrival, that I decided to go to his room and talk to him. Very forward and improper, I was sure, but I was determined. I had to speak to someone about Simon and Peter was the only outsider. I knew that he had been given a room on the ground floor, next to the Fletchers' suite. It was almost as though they wanted to be able to keep an eye on him twenty-four hours a day. That was certainly going to make it difficult to see him, but not impossible I was sure.

I had gone to my room straight from dinner and I allowed an hour to pass before setting out. Going to the door, I listened for any sounds outside before turning the handle. I was not entirely surprised to find that the door was locked. Once again, as on my first night, I was being made a prisoner in my own room. But this time I knew that the locked door was no barrier; I had both the handle of the candle snuffer and the old key from the Tradesmen's Door to take me out. In no time at all I was in the passageway. I listened. All was quiet; the castle was still.

I dared not take a light but felt my way along the corridor to the staircase landing. I leaned over the bannister and listened. Still no sound. My heart thumping, I stealthily made my way down the stairs. I had never before noticed how much they creaked. The sound now seemed to echo through the darkness, loud enough to wake the castle. I tried to put more of my weight onto the bannister rail, half sliding my way down the stairs.

I reached the bottom and flattened myself against the wall, listening. It was lucky I did. Just as I was about to move forward again a white-clad figure glided silently across the end of the hallway. I caught my breath. It was Babula, hurrying down the main corridor, intent on some mysterious errand. I waited several minutes to give him plenty of time to disappear.

A low murmur caught my attention. I crept to the end of the hallway and listened. The sound came from the sitting room. I realized that John and Cynthia were still up, probably having a final nightcap before going to bed. Perfect! I should be able to get into Peter's room without them knowing anything about it.

I tiptoed down the corridor, past the dining room and the library, to the junction of the cross-passageway. To the left was the kitchen; to the right the Fletchers' rooms and, I hoped, Peter's. Straight ahead was another entrance to the kitchen and, beyond it, a locked door that I believed led around to the East Tower. I was about to turn right when my luck ran out.

Down the corridor, behind me, the sitting room door opened and I heard Cynthia goading John to come to bed. Any minute one, or both, of them would step out and see me. I darted to the left and prayed that no one was in the kitchen. This time my luck held; the big room was dark and empty. I now dared not go down the back passage to the sitting room so, furtively, I crossed to the bottom of the stone stairs leading up the North Tower and to the servants' quarters. Pausing only a moment, I started up the steps, inwardly cursing that I had to abandon my quest to see Peter.

By then I was wide awake and getting used to moving through the murky darkness. I decided to do some exploring of that end of the castle, over the kitchen and the Fletchers' quarters. Perhaps there I could find further clues to Simon's whereabouts. My enthusiasm was a little dampened when, as I paused at the second floor landing – where I presumed Sara and the cook had their rooms – I felt something with a long tail scuttle across my feet. My throat went dry. A rat? I stifled a scream and hurried on up to the third floor.

By then it was quite dark and I was wishing I had brought a candle. Peering into the empty, dust-laden rooms, I found that so little light seeped in through the grimy windows that I could make out practically nothing at all. Then luck was with me again. Some of the rooms had apparently housed more servants at some time in the not-so-far-distant past. One or two of them were still partially furnished and, as I turned to leave one such room, my hand hit against something on top of a dresser. It was a candelabra, complete with candles. I quickly dug my hands into the pockets of my slacks and found a pack of matches. I had long since learned to always carry them with me. In no time I had struck a light and lit the candles. A squeaking and scampering in the far corners of the room greeted the flood of light and told me I was being left alone.

Looking about me I saw that, despite being servants' quarters, the room was still furnished in antiques, though sparingly. There was a four-poster bed, wardrobe, chest of drawers, and a stool. No dressing table or private bathroom here. Taking up the candelabra, I returned to the corridor and moved on. Other rooms were similarly furnished and little, gleaming eyes told me were similarly inhabited. There was no sign of disturbance of the dust anywhere; nothing to show that anyone had recently been there.

I arrived at the end of the passage and encountered another locked door. If my sense of direction was right, then this one led into the East Tower. I was trying to decide whether or not to try to unlock the door, when I heard a scream. It came from beyond the door; from somewhere high up in the tower, and I realized that this was the sound I had heard several times before. But from my own room, far removed from this corner of the castle, it had been faint and distant. I had attributed it to owls, or some other creatures of the night.

The scream came again. No owl but definitely human. Somehow it did not seem directly connected with Simon, though the possibility did pass through my mind. No, it seemed more like the voice of a much older person. As easily as it carried in the night air, there was a frailty to it. As I stood there, undecided whether or not to unlock the door and investigate, I heard the faint sound of footsteps on the stone steps behind the door. I couldn't make out whether they belonged to a man or a woman. I turned away and headed back towards my room.

During the following week I did manage to return to the room on the third floor . . . the one with all the clothes and boxes in it. Along with the red windbreaker I had previously discovered, I found a pair of sneakers, with paint on one; definite confirmation that they were the same items I had last seen in Simon's room. I left them there, but I did take the girl's yellow, lace-trimmed blouse back to my own room. Knowing now that something had befallen Simon, I was curious about the original owner of the blouse. I intended to question either Sara or Frau Brüning.

John was once more attentive to me, some of his previous attention having noticeably cooled during the first days of Peter's presence, but now John seemed to go out of his way to be nice to me. I know that Cynthia noticed it, and I couldn't help but notice the rapier-gleam in her eyes when she caught John leaning over to talk to me in the study. Peter, too, seemed perturbed by John's attentions to me, though why he should have been I had no idea.

I was ambivalent about both men. John was tremendously attractive and, I had to admit, his attention was flattering. Yet he frightened me. I would sometimes look up and catch a look in his eyes, as he stared at me from across the room, which sent shivers down my spine . . . and not the sort of shivers I got when he might affectionately squeeze my hand or gently smooth my hair.

Peter, too, I would catch staring at me. His smile was always so warm and friendly when I did catch his eye, that I could only like him for it. Yet, again, there were times when I would unobtrusively study him and find myself distrusting those thin, cruel-looking lips and pale cheeks. I noticed that, when thinking, he had a habit of tugging on his left ear. On someone else this might have been amusing, but with him I found it strangely ominous. I decided I had been lucky in being prevented from going to his room that night. I now wasn't sure that he was someone I should confide in. For the moment, at any rate, I would keep my own counsel.

I worked hard, typing new material for the screenplay and keeping up with correspondence for Cynthia. The latter was not difficult, since the weather had been too rough to allow the mail boat to call for more than a week. I discovered that I was locked in my room every night, yet the door was always unlocked again by the time Sara brought my morning breakfast tray. It didn't worry me, knowing that I had the means to get out whenever I wished, but I frequently wondered on the motive. The only likely conclusion I could reach was that Cynthia was responsible. Her strange possessiveness of her brother probably drove her to ensure that I did not attempt any midnight rendezvous with him!

I saw little of Babula, for which I was grateful. I had once mentioned to John about my room being searched that first week I was at Fletcher Castle. He seemed disturbed when I wondered who might have been responsible.

"Babula," he had finally said.

I looked at him blankly.

"Babula is a strange creature," he went on. "You say nothing was missing?"

"Right." I nodded.

"And you said it was a slip, or something, that first alerted you to the fact that your room had been searched?"

"A half-slip, yes. It had been refolded, as had most of my clothing."

"Underwear?"

"Yes."

He smiled. "I'll bet it was old Babula, getting his 'jollies' from handling your unmentionables."

I smiled back at him, a trifle uneasily. It certainly seemed a likely explanation, especially since nothing was missing. Yet on the other hand, it was an unsettling thought. What if 'old Babula' should want to get his 'jollies' handling more than just my underwear? I began to be grateful for Cynthia locking my door each night.

I had all but put Babula out of my mind when I left the dinner table one evening and went to my room. I had a slight headache and wanted to lie down. Just as I reached the top of the stairs and turned towards my room, I saw Babula disappearing down the far end of the corridor.

Strange, I thought. What was he doing there? My room was the only one occupied in that section of the house. I believed Babula had a room somewhere in the servants' quarters, though I wasn't absolutely sure. With trepidation I opened my door and looked in. Everything seemed normal until I saw Sirdah sitting on the end of the bed staring at me.

"Shoo! Scat! Get out!"

I took off my shoe and threw it at him. It missed. Disdainfully, and without hurrying, Sirdah got down from the bed, walked across to the door and, pausing only to give me a long look, trotted off down the hallway in the direction I had seen Babula take.

I was angry. I took off my other shoe and threw it across the room for no good reason. I slammed the door behind me and then checked the drawers of the bachelor chest. Everything seemed to be in order. I looked in the wardrobe. My dresses appeared undisturbed. I plumped myself down on the end of the bed.

Babula must have been in the room, I reasoned. How else could Sirdah have got in? But what did Babula want? Again, nothing was missing and, this time, it appeared that nothing had even been touched. So perhaps Babula had not been in my room? But then, how had Sirdah got in? I gave up and ran a bath. A good soak would help. Twenty minutes later I slipped into bed, after first bolting the door from the inside.

I lay awake for a long time. My headache had gone but I couldn't sleep. Every time I closed my eyes I saw either Babula's black eyes or Sirdah's red ones, staring at me. A slight scuffling in the corner reminded me that the mice were still about; strange since the cat was such a presence in the castle. Still, it was a big place. I would try to remember to get a trap from Frau Brüning the next morning.

There was a sudden bang from the bathroom. I sat up. Then something heavy slid, scraping, down the wall behind me and hit the head of the bed with a crash. The bed collapsed and I screamed as I rolled off on to the floor.

Chapter Thirteen

I must have hit my head on the bedside table as I fell, for a passed out. When I came to I heard someone pounding on my door. Both John and Peter were shouting to me from outside.

"Rebecca! Rebecca! Are you all right?"

"What happened in there? We can't get the door open!"

"She must have bolted it from the inside."

"Rebecca!"

"Rebecca! Can you hear me? Open the door."

Groggily I got to my feet. The room swayed and I held on to the little table until it steadied. My head throbbed. I looked at the broken bed. A heavy metal shield, studded with iron, had dropped from its place on the wall above the head of the bed. It had crashed down, right where my head would have been had I not sat up at the sound from the bathroom. I gave a silent prayer of thanks for noisy pipes.

"Rebecca! Are you all right?"

Peter sounded extremely worried. I moved unsteadily to the door.

"Yes. Yes, I think so. Just a minute."

I drew back the bolt and the door swung open. John rushed in and caught me up in his arms. Peter was right behind him.

"What in heaven's name happened?" asked John.

I savored the feel of being held so tightly to him. He seemed greatly agitated and I could feel the thumping of his heart through the soft smoothness of his velvet smoking jacket. I felt my own heart match this thumping and wondered if he was aware of it.

"My god! Look at this!"

Peter had moved across to survey the wreckage of the bed. His face was white as he turned to where John still held me.

"Rebecca, you – you could have been killed. How did this happen?" He seemed more upset by the accident than I was, which I thought surprising.

For the first time John shifted his attention from me to the bed.

"It's obvious that whatever held the shield up on the wall gave way," he said matter-of-factly. "Probably rotted through."

"What a strange place to hang such a heavy object in the first place," snapped Peter. He came across and examined my head. John – reluctantly, I thought – let go of me and went to look at the debris.

"You've got a nasty lump coming up, Becky," said Peter. His voice was soft and I felt a strange tingle when he called me "Becky". I hadn't been called that since I last saw Susan, just before I left Boston. His hand gently touched the growing lump on my forehead.

"Ouch!" I winced.

"Sorry! Here, you'd better come downstairs and let the good cook take a look at it. She knows something of accident treatment, I believe."

"How do you know that?" John's voice was sharp.

Peter glanced at him. "Oh, I was just chatting with her the other day."

"Hmm." John folded his arms, as he did when angry, and said nothing.

Peter took up my robe from the top of the chest and put it about my shoulders. Then, firmly taking my arm, he led me out of the room and along towards the staircase.

"I guess I must be accident prone," I said, trying to laugh, as we started down the stairs. The lump on my head had started to throb and I gingerly put up my hand to touch it.

"Take it easy now," said Peter. He glanced back up the stairs and then, his head close to mine, said, "What makes you think it was an accident?"

I stopped and stared at him.

"Come on." He pulled me on again, down the stairs.

"What do you mean?" I suddenly remembered my suspicions of Babula having been to my room that evening. Could he have been responsible? Did he want to kill me? I shuddered at the thought. But *why* would he want to?

"Ssh!" Peter squeezed my arm as John came hurrying down the stairs to catch up with us.

"I've sent Babula to get Frau Brüning," John said, reaching out and firmly taking my arm from Peter. "She'll meet us in the sitting room."

"Babula?" I gasped. Seeing Peter frown, as though some sort of warning, I added, "But where was he? I didn't see Babula about."

"He arrived just as you left the room," said John. "Heard your scream, as we did, and came to investigate."

Or to check on the results of his work, I thought.

We had hardly arrived in the sitting room, and I had been placed on the settee, when Frau Brüning hurried in from the back passageway carrying a tray. She looked most concerned and set about binding an ice pack over the swelling. I was surprised at how gently she treated me.

"Come along, Peter," said John. "You can help me see what can be done with that bed. Rebecca still has to have somewhere to sleep tonight."

The two men left the room.

"Thank you, Frau Brüning," I said. "That feels much better already. I suppose you heard what happened?"

She looked down and busied herself with putting scissors and bandages back on the tray.

"*Ja*," she finally said. "*Ja*. I heard." Then she looked up at me and I was surprised to see a moistness about her eyes. She looked very solemn and, I thought, almost frightened. She put her hand on my arm. "*Fraulein* Rebecca, go away from here. Please. Before it is too late."

I was amazed. What could she mean?

"But . . . Frau Brüning, . . ."

She raised her hand to silence me, got up, and hurried out of the room to return to the kitchen.

I sat quietly for a few moments, wondering what the cook could have meant. The martinet of the kitchen had seemed suddenly very human; almost motherly. Why was she asking me to leave Fletcher's Folly? Was it just because of the accident? Despite Peter's obvious suspicions, I still felt it could only have been that . . . an accident. After all, *why* would anyone want to kill me? Especially Babula. Unless – and here my heart skipped a beat – unless he was acting on someone else's orders. Cynthia's, perhaps? But again, why?

A new thought struck me. Where was Cynthia? It seemed that everyone else had been aroused by my experience. Why hadn't Cynthia put in an appearance? Perhaps it was simply that she was sound asleep. On reflection I remembered that she sometimes took sleeping pills. Yes, that was probably the explanation.

There was a tap on the door and then Sara's face peered around it. I smiled and she waved for me to follow her. I got up and together we went along the passage to the stairs, and then up to my room again. I presumed that John had sent her to get me. Back in my room I found that the fateful shield had been removed, and that the bed had been temporarily repaired by sliding the oak chest under the head, to take the place of the broken legs. Certainly sufficient repair to enable me to get some sleep that night.

I was surprised when Sara closed the bedroom door and bolted it, still on the inside with me. She then settled herself down in the armchair beside the door, obviously intending to stay the night.

"Sara," I sad. "You don't have to stay with me. I shall be all right now. You can go and sleep in your own bed."

She shook her head vigorously.

"Did someone tell you to stay with me?" I asked.

She nodded.

"John – Mr. Fletcher?"

She shook her head.

"Frau Brüning . . . or Peter?"

She nodded again, but I was not sure to which one. I decided to let it go at that. I pulled the top blanket off the bed and spread it over her. "There. You'll be all right, and so shall I."

She smiled at me and then closed her eyes like a dutiful child. I smiled too, and then went across to sink down thankfully, once more, on the bed. I hoped there would be no more excitement that night. But it took me quite a while to fall asleep. Frau Brüning's words kept coming back to me. "Go away from her. Please. Before it is too late."

Chapter Fourteen

I woke to find the morning sunlight steaming through the window and Sara standing beside the bed, tugging my arm. She must have been awake early and gone down to the kitchen, for there was my usual breakfast tray on the table beside me. Once she saw I was awake she would have gone running off back to the kitchen, but I restrained her. I made her sit down on the edge of the bed and share with me the hot buttered toast and marmalade. She sat there, swinging her legs, and humming some tuneless tune; a picture of contentment.

I still kept her in the room while I got up and dressed. Perhaps it was a delayed reaction to the previous night's emotion, but it felt good to have someone there with me. The lump on my head had gone down, thanks to Frau Brüning's ministrations, and I was able to dispense with the bandage and compress. I was sitting at the dressing table, combing my hair, when Sara suddenly became very agitated, running up and down the room and making strange little noises like whimpers.

"What is it, Sara? What's wrong?"

She stood still and looked at me. I saw that she was shaking all over as though shivering from cold. She pointed towards the wardrobe. I followed the direction she indicated and saw, where the door stood slightly open, the yellow, lace-trimmed blouse I had brought down from the room on the third floor. I went across and took it off its hangar.

"You recognize this, Sara?"

She covered her face with her hands.

"Sara! It's all right, Sara." I tried to remove her hands but she held them tight against her face. "Sara. Who was Julie?" I asked.

At the mention of the name, Sara started crying and ran up and down, bumping into furniture as she kept her face covered. I dropped the blouse on the bed and grabbed hold of her. She sobbed – great heaving sobs – as I held her.

"What on earth is the matter with Sara?"

I jumped at the sound of Cynthia's voice. Turning, I found her standing imperiously in the doorway, her hand resting idly on the door handle. I had no idea how long she had been there. Her gaze swept the room and came to a halt on the yellow blouse lying on the bed. Her face turned first white, and then a deep red.

"Where did you get that?" Her voice was low; scarcely audible. "Did Sara bring that here?" She spoke now through clenched teeth.

"Cynthia," I said. "Why . . ."

"Sara!" Cynthia suddenly shouted.

The poor little domestic broke from me and ran as fast as she was able out of the door, ducking under Cynthia's arm as she passed.

Cynthia shouted after her: "Get down to the kitchen *at once*, Sara! Frau Brüning has been looking for you."

She turned back to me, a trifle more composed. "I came to see how you were after last evening's . . . accident. I'm sorry I couldn't have got to see you then. I think – John thinks – perhaps you should take it easy today. I have plenty to keep me busy with Mr. Southwood. You rest up and we'll have plenty of work for you to catch up on tomorrow." She smiled, a trifle grimly I thought. "I would suggest either staying in your room or, perhaps, sitting outside down by the dock, if it's warm enough. I don't think," she added, meaningfully, "you should go wandering about the castle."

Before I could respond she went out, closing the door behind her.

The idea of having the day off both appealed to me and agitated me. I could enjoy being alone and relaxing, but at the same time it might have been better to have something to do; to occupy my mind. I was beginning to come up with a lot of questions to which I could not begin to find answers. I finally bundled up in a thick sweater and headed out, down to the dock.

The sun was shining but there was no warmth to it. I sat out on the dock itself, in a beach chair, listening to the water lap against the piers. I had taken a paperback novel with me but somehow I couldn't get into it. I kept looking up, across the wide expanse of water. There was still a brisk wind whipping up whitecaps, though I was sheltered from it where I sat. There was no sign of any boats out anywhere on the lake.

I turned my chair around so that I was facing the castle. Fletcher's Folly . . . what an appropriate name. And what folly it had been for me to come there, or so I was beginning to think. I had been looking for that "different" job; that bit of excitement. Well, the job itself might not be so different, but there was certainly excitement enough for a lifetime. Excitement enough to almost get me killed.

I thought again of the yellow blouse. Who was Julie? I remembered where I had heard the name before. Cynthia had called me Julie when John first introduced me. Did I really resemble this unknown girl? What had happened to her? Had she disappeared the same way Simon had? . . . or the way I might have done had I not been so lucky the previous night? I shivered. Perhaps some other young girl would one day have come across my old faded sweater, in that upstairs room. Perhaps Cynthia was so jealous she killed off every young girl John looked at? I laughed out loud. I was really letting my imagination run away with me. But even so, I thought, there was some sort of mystery to all of it. Simon *had* disappeared. And I had almost been killed. And there definitely was something strange about the yellow blouse and its original owner.

I had idly been looking over the outside of the castle as my mind rambled. Suddenly something caught my eye. High up, at one of the windows in the East Tower, I thought I saw a figure. It looked for all the world as though someone was standing in the dark, narrow window, looking down on me. I jumped to my feet and the figure vanished. Could I have been mistaken? I didn't think so. Perhaps it was Simon. Perhaps he was being held prisoner, though I couldn't for the life of me think why.

I sat down again and pretended to read my book, but I kept my eyes on the window in the tower. After a while I saw it again. A vague shape came to the window and looked down. It was too far for me to make out whether the figure was male or female. However, I somehow assumed it was a male, and also that it was an older person. Standing in the shadow as he was, I couldn't even make out whether his hair was grey, white, or what. Who could it be? Certainly neither Simon nor Julie. Who, then? And what was he doing in the tower? Was he a prisoner, I wondered?

The figure faded back into the room and, looking up to see what might have disturbed him, I saw John coming down the path towards me. He looked the aristocratic gentleman, with a green, paisley cravat tucked into his pale yellow, round-necked sweater. His tan colored slacks, over casual suede shoes, suggested jodhpurs and I half expected to see him swinging a riding crop! I felt happy to see him. He called out as he approached.

"Rebecca! How are you doing?"

"Hi, John. I'm fine, thanks."

"Bump is all deflated, I see."

He kissed me lightly on the temple, where the skin was beginning to turn; the start of a massive black-and-blue. I thrilled to his touch.

"The bump is gone, yes," I said. "But I'm beginning to break out in glorious Technicolor."

He laughed and dropped easily down to sit on the dock at my feet.

"I'm glad you are following doctor's orders and taking it easy today."

"Oh, I didn't need much persuading." I laughed.

John suddenly turned serious. "I really am sorry that such a terrible thing should have happened. And to you of all people, Rebecca."

"Don't be silly, John. It was just a weird accident." I wished I could really be sure of that.

"Yes, I know." He smiled. "And 'all's well that ends well', eh? All the same, it was stupid of me not to think of the possible hazards of decorating the walls with hefty war shields. Do you forgive me?" He looked up at me with his "little boy" look, and my heart melted.

"There's nothing to forgive, John." I said softly.

He took my hand and squeezed it. We sat in silence for a while. I felt very happy; all thoughts of falling shields, missing people, and figures at windows gone from my mind. My fantasizing had just progressed to where I saw myself as a medieval lady seated with her gallant crusader knight beside her, before their castle, when John broke in.

"You know," he said, trying to sound light, "I wouldn't place too much trust in that Southwood, if I were you."

"Peter?" I said, surprised.

"Yes. Peter."

"But, why ever not?"

"Oh, you know what these movie types are like," he said, an artificial smile on his face.

No I didn't, I thought. I had never met one before . . . and I just might like to have the chance to find out. "Well," I said aloud. "I never seem to find myself alone with him, so I guess I don't have to worry too much."

It was true. I never did get to be alone with Peter. It wasn't so much that I wanted to be. It was just that, on reflection, I realized I was never *allowed* to be. John seemed to watch over us like a hawk. Could he be jealous, I wondered? If so, it must run in the family, the way Cynthia was so jealous of me.

As if in answer to my thoughts, Cynthia herself appeared in the castle entranceway and called to John. He didn't seem too delighted to see her and, reluctantly, got to his feet.

"I guess the old girl has another problem." He sighed. "I'd better go and see what it is. Now don't you sit out here too long, Rebecca. Don't want you catching cold." He turned to go. "And remember what I said about Mr. Peter Southwood."

He strode away up the path towards the impatient Cynthia. Together they went into the castle.

It was almost an hour later that I returned to the house. There had been no further sign of the figure at the window in the East Tower. The temperature had dropped and I decided to go in and do a little reading in the library. I was approaching the door, and almost had my hand on the door handle, when I heard voices coming from inside the room. They were angry voices and they belonged to John and Cynthia. I had no intention of eavesdropping, but I couldn't help overhearing some of what was said.

"And you agreed," said John. "Just remember that. You agreed."

"I must have been out of my mind." Cynthia snorted. "I had more than enough with the last one."

"Well, this one's different . . . and important. Don't you forget that! Damned important. Could be the final answer."

"Final answer! I can't see any finality in sight at the moment."

"We've got to be patient." John sounded calmer. "You have to curb your jealousy and remember that we're both together."

"Together?" Cynthia shouted again. "Why is it that the husband always has the fun and the wife the worry? Eh? Answer me that!"

"Cynthia!" John spoke grimly. "There is good reason for the way things are, as you well know. *I* am in charge, just you keep that in mind! What I say, goes. Don't you forget it!"

I moved away and headed for the kitchen to find Frau Brüning and to thank her for the previous evening's relief. I didn't understand what John and Cynthia were arguing about and I didn't want to know. So long as they weren't arguing over me, for any silly reason, I had no need to worry.

Chapter Fifteen

The next two or three days passed uneventfully. John, Peter, and Babula managed, with much struggling, to move the broken bed out of my room and to replace it with another from one of the unused room. The new one was a similar, though sturdier, four-posted bed but without a canopy. Although not quite as comfortable as the old bed, it might keep the whole upper floor from falling on me.

I did not get a chance to speak to Sara again about Julie, the owner of the blouse. In fact Sara seemed to avoid me, though that might have been my imagination. Similarly, I was not able to question Frau Brüning about her warning. I did try to get alone with Peter though, and once almost succeeded. I spotted him going into the library when I was on my way to the study. I slipped back along the passage and into the library after him.

"Rebecca!" He seemed surprised to see me, though not unhappy.

"Hi, Peter! Yes, I'm being very forward."

"What do you mean?"

"Well in case you haven't noticed, we are never allowed to be alone together. So I've come in here after you for just that reason."

He grinned. "Great! And yes, I had noticed. And you're right when you say 'never allowed'. It's more than just coincidence." He put down the book he was holding and came over to me, by the door. "Rebecca, I've been wanting a chance to talk to you. It's very important."

"You sound serious," I said.

"I am. First of all, Becky. Do you trust John?"

I looked at him. "Not trust John? But why ever not? I would have thought Cynthia would have been the one you would warn me against." I smiled. "And you know what's funny?"

"What?"

"Only the other day John was warning me not to trust you."

He smiled, but without humor.

Suddenly the door behind me opened and John himself came hurrying into the room.

"You see?" said Peter.

"See what?" asked John.

"See Cynthia," I said quickly. "That's what I have to do. Is she in the study, John?"

He nodded, his eyes on Peter.

"Thanks." I hurried out and along the passage to the study.

Cynthia was sitting in her usual high-backed chair, spilling cigarette ash all over the papers scattered before her. She barely glanced up as I entered.

"Have you received any mail recently?" I asked.

"No, Rebecca. The water's been much too rough for the mail boat to come round the islands."

"Does that happen often?" I asked, taking up a pile of papers to be collated.

"Uhu." Cynthia grunted. "Especially this time of year. Can be a damned nuisance when you're waiting for something. Lucky thing all I get is rejections." She laughed grimly.

"Not any more," I said. "Once this movie is out all sorts of publishers will be after you."

"You think so?" She raised a quizzical eyebrow.

"I'm sure of it. In fact even before the movie is released they'll probably be after you. Just as soon as word gets around that they're making it."

"Hmm! I wonder." She seemed pleased.

I took the papers to my desk and started separating the different copies. We worked in silence for a while, until Cynthia suddenly said: "Where did that yellow blouse come from? The one that was on your bed the other day."

I was taken by surprise. I had quite forgotten the incident of two or three days before. I now presumed that she had questioned Sara and found that she was not responsible for its appearance. I couldn't very well admit that I had unlocked the passage door and gone prowling around the forbidden parts of the castle.

"Er, it . . . it was in my wardrobe."

"In the wardrobe? I thought that had been thoroughly cleaned out," she said, speaking more to herself than to me.

I had not actually lied. All I had said was that the blouse was in my wardrobe ... which it was, just before I took it out and laid it on the bed.

Admittedly I hadn't explained how it came to be in my wardrobe in the first place, and I was grateful that now it looked as though I wouldn't have to.

"Well, never mind," said Cynthia. "It belonged to – to a young girl who worked here for a while. Just before you came, as a matter of fact."

"Julie?" I asked.

Cynthia's head snapped up, her eyes wide. "How do you know her name?" she hissed.

"That's the name embroidered on the blouse," I said, surprised by her reaction.

"Oh! Oh yes, of course." She smiled at me, and the smile became fixed. I thought that her eyes looked strange; slightly glazed. "Of course, dear." She shivered slightly and rubbed her arms. "My, but it's turned cold. Would you do me a favor, dear? Would you run down to my room and fetch me my cardigan? It's right there on the chair by the door."

"Why of course, Cynthia," I said. I was surprised. Never before had I been anywhere near the Fletcher apartment. I got up and went to the door. "Be right back," I said.

"Thank you, Julie," she said.

As I was about to turn the corner at the end of the main corridor, I heard a door open ahead of me. It was the door to the kitchen. I stopped before turning the corner, to see who was there. Sara came out carrying a tray on which was a covered dish and eating utensils. Instead of turning towards me, as I expected, she turned away to face the door forming the end of the passageway. Balancing the tray on her knee, she fumbled with a key and unlocked the door. Without noticing me watching her, Sara went quickly through the door, closing it behind her.

Where on earth would she be going, I wondered? Surely that was the door that led to the East Tower. Then I remembered the old man's figure I had seen at the window, high up in the tower. Could she be taking food to him? If so, then who was he, and why was he kept hidden away?

I moved on around the corner and down the passageway to Cynthia's and John's rooms. I half expected to find the door locked but it opened easily to my touch. I found myself in a large, bright sitting room with a bay window to look out at the morning sun. The room was lavishly furnished with mixed-period chairs, tables, and a settee. There was a comfortable-looking Queen Anne wing chair near the window and I could picture John sitting in it. A matching footstool was beside it; a newspaper and a couple of magazines on that, probably where John had dropped them.

I could picture Cynthia in the Gainsborough armchair across from John's . . . if, indeed, it was his. Behind this was a Chippendale flapped dining table with four matching chairs. There was a bureau-bookcase in one corner of the room and a sideboard in another. A door led through to what I presumed were the bedrooms. I saw Cynthia's cardigan, as she had said, draped over the arm of a Hepplewhite armchair beside the door. Before I picked it up I gave-in to the urge to run across and peek through the bedroom door. I was surprised to find just one large bedroom – again with a bay window in the east wall – and even more surprised to discover just one large double bed. Perhaps, then, both John and Cynthia did not sleep there? Perhaps John had a bedroom elsewhere? In the East Tower, perhaps? But the doors to a double wardrobe stood open and there, alongside Cynthia's dresses and skirts, hung John's suits. Perplexed, I turned away, picked up Cynthia's cardigan, and returned to the study.

It was none of my business I knew, but it puzzled me. Surely brother and sister, as adults, did not usually sleep together? And if not, then whichever one slept in that bed, where did the other one sleep? They both retired to those rooms at night, I knew. Really, it was none of my business!

Late that afternoon I found myself alone in the study. Cynthia and Peter had gone to the library and Babula had summoned John away on some mysterious errand. I worked quite happily for an hour or so. The time always seemed to pass quickly when I had something with which to occupy myself. I typed up to date with the screenplay and then moved across to the big table to collate the copies. Peter's briefcase stood, open, on the corner of the table and I went to move it. Clumsily, I didn't get a good grip on it and dropped it on the floor, spilling out papers in all directions over the rug. Silently cursing the fact that I also broke a fingernail, I knelt to clear up the mess.

As I gathered up the papers, and straightened them before replacing them, I noticed the corner of a white piece of paper sticking out from the lining of the briefcase lid. Apparently at some time in the past whatever it was must have slipped behind the lining and now, through my dropping the case, it had been shaken into view again. I took hold of the corner and pulled. Out came a small business card.

The card was for a law firm: Phelps, Cotterell, Bryant, and Martine. Their offices were in New York. What intrigued me about the card, however, was the name listed in the bottom corner as "Associate": Peter Southwood. What did this mean, I wondered? Why would Peter be listed as a member of a law firm when he was at Fletcher's Folly as a motion picture company's representative? Then I thought about what must have happened. Peter had probably worked for the lawyers at some time in the past, perhaps immediately prior to the movie job. The business card had obviously got stuck behind the lining quite some time before. On an impulse, I slipped the card into the pockets of my jeans, closed up the briefcase, and put it on one of the chairs. I then got on with my collating. I had almost finished when Cynthia and Peter returned from the library.

"I just think you need a little more background information to help establish the character," Peter was saying.

"He's not one of the leads," Cynthia responded.

"No, I know that. However, he is important to the development of the plot."

"Well what would you suggest? We could make him a carpenter . . . or a tailor?"

"No, no. Something a little more professional, I think."

"What do you say, Rebecca?" asked Cynthia. "Any ideas?"

"Who are we talking about?"

"The character Sam Parker," said Peter. "You remember? In Cynthia's story he's the one who recognizes the stolen car."

"Oh, yes," I said. "So you want a profession for him? How about a bank teller?"

"Hm. Has possibilities," Peter mused.

"No," said Cynthia. "I don't know anything about banks. I couldn't write convincingly."

I had a sudden idea. "Okay," I said. "Then make him a lawyer."

"I don't know anything about lawyers either."

I smiled. "Well that's no problem. Peter could help you."

I thought I saw Peter's jaw drop but I must have been mistaken, for he grinned broadly.

"Cross that off too," he said. "I don't know anything about lawyers."

My jaw dropped.

Chapter Sixteen

I woke up worried about Sara. Why I should have been I didn't really know. The previous evening I had again caught a glimpse of her carrying a tray through the East Tower door. Later, from my room, I had heard those strange, unexplained, far-distant screams. I was now certain that they came from the East Tower and presumed that the man at the window, whoever he was, was responsible for them. He must be the one Sara's food trays were for.

I glanced at my watch on the bedside table. Twenty minutes after seven o'clock. Sara usually brought me my breakfast by seven; never later than seven fifteen. I got up and threw on my robe. But for the sound of the wind whistling around the battlements high above, there was no noise in the castle as I hurried down the stairs and along to the kitchen. Frau Brüning looked up as I entered.

"*Acht*! I thought it was that lazy girl."

"Sara?"

"*Ja.*"

"Then you haven't seen her this morning?"

"*Nein.*" She shook her head.

"Have you checked her room?" I asked. "Perhaps she's ill."

"I don't have time to go running around after the help," she said. "She was all right last night. She has probably just overslept. I'll wake her up all right when she does show up!"

I was not happy. There was a deep gnawing in the base of my stomach that told me all was not well.

"Which is her room? I'll go up and check on her myself," I said.

The cook shrugged. "Please yourself. You won't get me running up and down stairs after a lazy good-for-nothing like that. She has third room on left on second floor."

I thanked her and started up the North Tower stairs. It didn't take me long to reach the second floor and the third door on the left. I found it unlocked.

The room was empty. It was very small and contained only a bed, chest of drawers, and a wardrobe. I looked around at the faded green wallpaper, the cracked washbasin and jug on top of the chest, and the colorless curtains shrouding the small, high window. Not much of a room to call home, especially for a lonely little creature like Sara, I thought. I vowed to spend my next day off making the room brighter and more lively. Perhaps I could even talk John into giving her a larger room. Goodness knows, there were enough empty ones in the castle. Then I realized that the bed had not been slept in.

My first thought was that she had run away. Then I reminded myself that we were on an island and there was a near-gale blowing that hadn't let up for three days. No, something must have happened to her.

I returned to the kitchen to find Frau Brüning about to take the Fletchers their breakfast. She was angrily muttering to herself that this was not her job, and that she'd really teach Sara a lesson when she did show up.

"Frau Brüning!" I called. "Sara is not in her room and it doesn't look as though her bed has been slept in."

The old woman looked up sharply. The mutterings stopped, leaving her mouth agape.

"What do you mean, 'not slept in'?" The sharpness of her tone told me she had some deep, inner feelings for the little domestic after all.

"That's right. I'd say she hasn't been in her room since yesterday."

"Oh! *Mein Gott!*"

"Take that tray on to the Fletchers," I said, unconsciously assuming control. "Tell them what I've just told you, and have them get Babula to start searching for her. You and he know the castle better than I do, so you start inside. I'm going to get dressed and go down to the dock to start looking there."

She nodded and I pushed her out of the door and then hurried out myself.

In a very short time I was dressed and, with my topcoat pulled tightly about me, and rain hat on my head, started down the front path to the dock. The howling wind tugged at me and it was all I could do to move against it. Through the driving rain I could see there was no one on the dock itself so I made for the boathouse.

As I opened the door a sudden gust took it out of my hand and slammed it back against the boathouse wall. I moved inside the gloomy structure and, for a moment, was able to straighten up and enjoy a respite from the wind. The building was low and long, sticking out into the lake. Little light entered from the water and I nervously looked about in the deep, dark shadows around me. A large, old-fashioned ChrisCraft motorboat, of the nineteen-thirties, moved restlessly against its moorings. Beside it was a modern, fiberglass, outboard boat; the one Peter had arrived in.

Above them, from the sail loft, stray ropes and canvas hung down like some great, dismal, bridal veil. In one corner a decrepit ladder disappeared up into the gloom above; the ancient means of access to the loft. Most of the ladder's rungs had long since rotted away and I gave a silent prayer of thanks that I wouldn't need to clamber up to investigate that space.

Along one wall an old canoe, its canvas rotted, shared space with an assortment of oars, poles, paddles, ropes, and – incongruously – a supermarket shopping cart. Some bags of cement and a wheelbarrow concluded the boathouse contents. I braced myself to plunge back outside, into the clawing wind.

Where could Sara have gone, I wondered, as I fought my way back towards the castle? As I drew nearer, its great gray bulk, turned almost black by the wetness of the wind, towered over me like some giant predator. Despite the early morning hour I could only dimly make out the East Tower off to my right. I had a sudden thought; a sense of intuition . . . and foreboding. I turned away from the castle entrance and moved off towards the tower.

It didn't take long to find what I somehow knew I would. She lay crumpled, one leg twisted under her. The wind must have caught her, for Sara lay some distance back from the tower, at the base of a massive maple tree, her head smashed on a rock. I knelt down beside her and wept.

"What a tragedy," said Cynthia, lighting a fresh cigarette from the stub of the previous one. "What a tragedy! Why, I was so fond of poor little Sara. So very fond of her."

Peter murmured something and Cynthia reached through her smoke to take a sip from her whiskey glass, on the table beside her. I looked at her. Never, in the time I had been at Fletcher's Folly, had I known Cynthia to speak affectionately of Sara, or to speak of her at all for that matter.

The three of us sat in the sitting room, glumly awaiting the call to dinner. The day had been a long one. I had been more upset by the tragedy of Sara's death than I ever would have expected. Although I knew that I was not responsible for it, I couldn't help wondering whether the incident of the yellow blouse was in any way connected; had in any way contributed to her death? Not that I had any proof that Sara had been murdered. Indeed, the more I studied Cynthia the more I had to push such thoughts from my mind.

John had insisted that Sara must have gone up to the top of the tower and either slipped or been blown off.

"Had she ever gone up there before?" I asked.

"Oh, yes." He nodded, grimly. "If I'd warned her once I'd warned her a dozen times. I told her it was dangerous up there . . . the top battlements of the tower have not been finished off, you see. Some of the rim has no parapet, so it would be easy to fall over."

"Even accidentally," Peter had added, sardonically. John ignored him.

"But *why* would Sara go up there?" I repeated, thinking of her mysterious errands with the trays of food.

John shrugged. "I think she just likes – liked – the view."

"In the middle of the night?" asked Peter.

"We don't know it was the middle of the night. She might have fallen yesterday evening, or even early this morning." John thought for a moment, then added: "She might have gone up there to watch the sunrise."

"Uh-oh!" Peter shook his head. "She didn't fall this morning."

"How do you know?"

"Rigor mortis."

"What's that supposed to mean?"

Peter looked uncomfortable, as though he had said more than he intended. But he was committed. "The body begins to stiffen anywhere between one and six hours after death." He sighed. "It might then remain rigid for anywhere from twelve to forty-eight hours. When Rebecca found her Sara was as stiff as a board, so she had to have been dead for longer than from sunrise."

Chapter Seventeen

I looked at Peter, sitting in the sitting room, his hands flat in front of him, staring at his fingers. How had he known the details of rigor mortis? He had said that he got the information from a movie script. I suppose that was possible, yet . . . somehow it didn't seem probable.

"What happened to Sara's body?" I asked.

Both Cynthia and Peter looked up in surprise.

"What do you mean?"

"I mean, shouldn't the authorities – the police, or whomever – shouldn't they be notified?"

"I think John did that," said Cynthia. "He said he was sending the body across to the mainland. I expect Babula took care of it."

My eyes caught Peter's. Through the thick, stone walls of the castle we could hear the wind still moaning. It hadn't let up all day. There was no way any boat could have left the island.

After dinner I excused myself and quickly left the dining room. Instead of going upstairs to my room, I headed down the corridor to the door to the East Tower. I had to do a little checking for myself. I first slipped into the kitchen and helped myself to a candle and holder, lighting it from the fire. Thankfully Frau Brüning was not there, probably being on her way to and from the dining room.

The locked door at the end of the passage yielded easily to my key. I quickly moved through and closed the door behind me. Holding my candle high, I saw a narrow passageway to my right, much like the one from the sitting room to the kitchen. It obviously followed the outer wall to the junction of the castle and the East Tower. In no time I reached the end and found before me a wide stone stairway, ascending into the tower. To my left was a door, which I remembered as being the one leading outside; the one with the bear trap before it.

To my right there was another door, which puzzled me for a moment. In my mind I ran over the floor plan of the castle in this, the east, corner. I quickly realized that the only place this door could lead was directly into the Fletchers' apartment. That was something I hadn't expected. Suppose I was up in the tower and Cynthia or John came up? How would I explain myself? I decided to face that when, and if, it happened. I started up the stairs.

At the first landing I found three empty rooms. They were laden with dust, which tickled my nose and made me sneeze. The next floor was equally abandoned. I shuddered a little as I saw traces of mice, or rats, in the room and I almost dropped the candle when a bat flew erratically past me out of one room into which I peered. The stairway was cold and damp and I clutched my cardigan close about me with my free hand. I could hear the whistle of the wind around the outside of the tower. Glancing again at the dust-laden rooms, I realized something . . . the stairway itself was *not* dusty.

Obviously the stairs up into the East Tower were used frequently. If they were not then they would have been as dusty as the empty rooms, and would certainly have shown Sara's footprints in the dust. But they were clear, as though well used and regularly swept. Dirty and dusty in the corners and at the edges, to be sure, yet as clear as any of the used corridors in the main body of the castle. How could that be, I wondered? Who frequented the tower? Cynthia? John? I moved on upwards, hoping to find out.

As I got higher a strange dread crept over me. My legs seemed to grow heavy the higher I climbed; much more so than would have been natural from the simple exertion of climbing stone stairs. My breathing became strenuous; I could feel my heart thumping as I drew deep, gasping breaths. I made frequent stops to lean against the cold, clammy wall. It was almost as though some strange, invisible force was working against me. But I was determined and struggled on. What would I find at the top? What was the strange mystery of the forbidden tower?

At the next-to-the-top floor I found a door to one of the rooms, but it was locked. There was a heavy, modern, well-oiled padlock on the door and it could not be opened with my trusty key. I put my ear to the door and listened carefully. For a moment I could almost swear that I could hear someone breathing on the other side. But I couldn't be certain. This must be the room where I had seen the figure at the window, I realized. I tapped on the door and called: "Simon!" There was no reply.

After checking that the other two rooms were empty, I went on up the final flight to the top floor. There I found only one door, which must have been to a very large room. Probably the one with the big picture window I had seen from the ground, I guessed. Once again the door was sealed with a new padlock. As I stood with my ear to this door, listening, I was almost overpowered by a tremendous sense of evil. It seemed to flow over me and all around me, like a shroud. I pushed myself away from the door, gasping for breath.

Suddenly a horrible, nerve-jarring scream echoed through the tower. I almost screamed myself and dropped the candle. It spluttered and went out. The scream echoed and re-echoed around the tower walls. It seemed to come from the room below me, where I thought I might have heard someone breathing. It must have been the old man I saw at the window. But who was he? Why was he kept locked in that room, so high in the tower? What could possible cause him to scream as though his very soul was being tortured?

I braced myself and determined to go back down and try to speak to him through the door. I felt about, found the candle and, taking matches from my pocket, relit it. I started down the stairs but, as I neared the lower landing, I was horrified to hear footsteps coming up from the lower levels. I turned and, trying not to make a sound, raced back up to the top floor. I stumbled on the top step and fell hard, on my knees, rolling across the cold, stone floor. The candle once again went flying but I was quickly able to grope around and retrieve it. I painfully got to my feet and one more time relit the candle, only too aware of the fact that someone was coming up the stairs. What should I do? Where could I hide?

As if in answer to my silent prayers, the landing was suddenly lit by a flash of lightning. I hadn't noticed any windows on the landing but then I realized that the lightning flash had come down a narrow flight of steps in the far corner. Of course! They had to lead up to the roof; the battlements of the tower. But John had said that Sara had fallen from there. The sound of a step on the stairs behind me put an end to my hesitation. I moved quickly but quietly across to the stone stairs and went up.

An old wooden door at the top of the steps hung open. It seems that was what had allowed me to see the lightning. I left my candle – once again extinguished – on the top step behind me and moved out onto the roof of the tower. The rain had stopped but the wind still howled and all about me I could see the lightning flashing down at the lake. Heavy black clouds boiled in the sky, allowing only fleeting glimpses of the round, almost full moon.

I crouched low against the wind. If Sara had come up here alone, I thought, she could easily have been blown over the edge. I could see where the castellated parapet had been completed around only half of the tower's circumference. The rest was open at the edge. But – I suddenly realized – the open portion was at the *back* of the tower, away from the side from which Sara fell. If Sara had fallen accidentally she would have had to be standing up on top of the three-foot high parapet. And why would she ever do a thing like that?

My thoughts were interrupted by a sudden glow of light. I saw that the center of the roof was covered by a large skylight for the room beneath . . . the top floor's locked room. Whoever had come up the stairs behind me must have entered that room, his candelabra now lighting up the night sky. His? . . . or hers?

Chapter Eighteen

I crept to the edge of the skylight and looked down. It was difficult to make out much. The glass was slightly greenish in color, thick and bubbled, making it translucent. It was obviously there solely as a means of receiving light, and not as a window for viewing.

Squinting my eyes, I could vaguely make-out the layout of the room. It seemed almost bare of furniture. The center of the floor seemed to be painted with a strange design. It looked like a large circle – or two or three concentric circles, close together – with a star shape in the middle. The outer circle must have been all of ten or twelve feet in diameter. It looked as though there were words written around the circle, but I couldn't make them out. A small table stood in the center of the star design. On it I could make out a book, a candelabra holding a number of red candles, and what looked for all the world like a sword.

As I looked, a figure moved into my field of vision. Dressed in a long, flowing, scarlet robe, with a hood over the head, I couldn't tell whether it was man or woman. The figure moved around the edges of the circle, lighting candles standing at the four quarters of the floor design. These candles were black.

Moving then to the table in the center, this figure lit the red candles and also something in what looked like a gold box. When the figure started to swing the box, on a chain, I decided it must be an incense-burner. I had seen such a thing in films, usually at a Roman Catholic church, or similar. Pressing my ear to the skylight, I could – with the occasional lulls in the whistling wind – barely make out the sound of someone singing or chanting. Not clearly enough to recognize the voice, though it did seem to be a male one. Surely not John, I thought? Then I remembered Babula. I never could discover where his room was and had long suspected that it might be in the tower. Perhaps this was it? Strange ceremonies late at night certainly seemed more befitting Babula than John.

An ear-splitting crash of thunder directly overhead made me cry out. Lightning seemed suddenly to be concentrated all around the tower. Vivid flashes lit up the outside of the castle and from the tower I could look down on the top of it, seeing it stretching away into the night. The East Tower stretched high above the main building; higher then the North Tower which, in the repeated flashes, I could make out off to my right. It was almost as if the activities of the red-clad figure below had drawn the storm to this tower.

I looked down again to see the figure moving around the circle, swinging his censer and chanting. Having gone around three times, he returned to the center table and opened the book resting there. There then followed a long period during which time he seemed to be reading aloud from the book. He spoke in a strong, stern voice, though not loud enough that I could make out much, between the thunder, the wind, and the renewed rain. He seemed to be demanding something of someone, though I was certain he was alone in the room. He appeared angry and would read long lists of words, or names, as though the repeating of them would give him special authority.

With the rain starting again, and intensifying, I was quickly soaked to the skin. I wondered if it might be possible to slip down the stairs and past the door while he was completing his ritual. I knew I had to chance it or I would catch my death of cold. I ducked into the doorway, found my candle, and crept quietly down towards the upper landing.

At the foot of the narrow roof stairs, I paused and listened. No sound came from the door to the room where the ritual was being performed. I felt a sneeze coming on but managed to suppress it. I really needed to get back to my own room, and the sooner the better. I stepped off the bottom step on to the landing floor.

There came a tremendous clap of thunder overhead and, at the same time, a sheet of lightning flashed down the stairs. It seemed as though the lightning passed within an inch of me, for I felt the intense heat and was almost blinded by the brightness. I screamed but mercifully the sound was drowned by the continuing thunder. As the lightning struck the inner wall of the tower I was thrown across the landing and ended with my head hanging over the stones steps leading on down from the tower. Below me the poor creature locked in the room renewed his screaming and continued as though he would never stop. I knew that I had to get out of there before the figure in the red robe came out to investigate.

It took me a moment to gather enough strength to move but I finally managed to drag myself down the stairs, leaning against the rough stone wall as I went. I reached the next level before I heard the door above me open. I hurried past the locked door, which now reverberated as the screaming man inside pounded on it with his fists. The sound echoed through the unholy tower. I hurried on, hearing footsteps descending the stairs behind me. They stopped at the imprisoned man's door, as I knew they would, and I heard a muttered cursing as the padlock was opened. As dearly as I would have wished to discover the identities of both the men, I hurried on through the darkness. I had lost my candle and trusted to feeling the wall to guide me. I felt weak and knew I must get to my room as soon as possible.

The next three days I spent in bed recovering from one of the worst colds I have ever suffered. Everyone assumed it was a delayed reaction to my going out into the storm to search for Sara. I was too weak to say otherwise, not that I would have done so anyway. Cynthia was very good and very considerate. She would bring me my lunch on a tray and would sit and talk to me or read me her latest writing of the screenplay. I would probably have been very grateful for these visits had Sirdah not always accompanied her. The cat would jump up on the bottom corner of my bed and sit there staring at me the whole time Cynthia was with me. His red eyes would never leave my face, gazing at me unblinkingly at though reading and absorbing all that was in my mind.

"Does Sirdah go everywhere with you?" I once asked.

"Sirdah? Heavens, no! Sirdah is a very independently-minded individual. He goes where he wants to go; and does *not* go where he'd rather not."

"An 'individual'?" I said. "Funny, I've never before heard anyone refer to a cat as an individual. You make him sound almost human, Cynthia"

"Well, he almost is . . . or so it seems," she added hastily.

"He is very close to you."

"Oh, yes. He is a part of me."

Before I could ask what she meant by that cryptic remark, John came into the room. He had looked in once or twice before but I had been too sick to fully appreciate his presence. Beginning to feel decidedly better, I hoped he would stay for a while.

"How's the invalid today?"

"I'm fine." I laughed. "And no invalid. I shall be up and about tomorrow, you'll see."

"I hope so," he said.

His voice was tender and I felt drawn to those fascinating gray eyes. Suddenly I longed to touch him; to reach out and take his hands in mine; to be close to him.

"Won't you stay and talk awhile?" I asked, hoping not to sound too presumptuous. "That is, if you haven't anything else to attend to right now?"

"What could be more important than comforting the sick?" He smiled.

Cynthia got up. "Well, *I* have things to do," she said, briskly, and headed towards the door. Sirdah jumped down from the bed and followed after her. "Don't keep Julie too long, John," she said over her shoulder. "She still needs her rest, you know." She went out, closing the door unnecessarily loudly behind her.

"Oh, dear!" I said. "I do hope I haven't upset Cynthia, asking you to stay and talk."

"Not at all. It's me she's angry at." He spoke bitterly, moving the chair Cynthia had just vacated a little closer to the bed. He sat down and smiled at me. "But then, that's nothing new."

He reached out and took my hand in his. His touch sent flutters up and down my spine and I dug my teeth into my lower lip to keep from blushing like a schoolgirl.

"Tell me, " he said. "What have you been doing with yourself these last two or three days?"

"Well, the first two I did nothing but feel sorry for myself," I said. "It's really only today that I've started to look around and think of anything other than my own misery."

"Do you have everything you want? Is there anything I can get for you?"

"No. No, nothing. Thank you, John."

"How about a book to read?" His two hands cupped mine and gently caressed it. I had trouble concentrating.

"What? Oh, a book? Er – er, yes. Yes, that's a good idea." I had a thought. "There is a book I'd like to look at while I'm stuck here in bed. If you wouldn't mind, John?"

"Of course not. I'll be happy t get it for you. Which one is it?"

"I noticed it in the library the other week," I said. "And thought the title sounded fascinating. It's called *The Book of Sacred Magic of Abra-Melin the Mage.*"

For a moment John's hands gripped mine very tightly. Then he let go. He looked me straight in the eyes but this time I felt no magnetic pull.

"Do you know the book?" I asked. I let my hand lay where it was on the bedspread, hoping he might take it up again. He did not.

"Yes." He nodded. "Yes. I think I know the one you're referring to. Tell me, why do you want to look at that?"

"Oh, I don't know." I shrugged. "It was just that the title caught my eye and I wondered what it could possibly be about. What *is* it about, John? Do you know? Have you read it?"

"As the title says, it's about magic."

"You mean, pulling rabbits out of hats, and card tricks, and all that sort of thing?" I was disappointed. But not for long.

"Not at all."

John got up and walked over to the window. He stood silently for a moment, looking out. I noticed that the weather, outside, was finally nice again. It even looked as though the sun was trying to break through the clouds.

"Magic – real magic – is a practice." He stood, still staring out of the window "A practice that can be extremely dangerous."

"Dangerous?"

He didn't seem to hear me.

"Ceremonial magic is an ancient art; some call it a science. It has been practiced for hundreds of years. In all those centuries it has claimed many victims." He paused, and straightened up. "Yet some – some of the Masters of the Art – have done extremely well by it. Some have the ability, the knowledge, to use the *Art Magical* as it was meant to be used. To manipulate the Forces and have them do . . . " He paused a moment and turned to look at me. "*The Book of Sacred Magic* is an old *grimoire*; an ancient work written by a famous fifteenth century magician named Abra-Melin. It is a complete book of instructions for those who know how to read it. It is a Key to Power." In his eyes I caught a glimpse of red, reminding me of Sirdah's eyes.

"How do you use such power; such forces?" I asked, really curious, though seeing the change that had come over John, I wished I had never mentioned the book. Yet despite a growing sense of uneasiness, even of fear, I pursued the subject. It struck me that there might be some connection between what John was saying and the ceremony of the scarlet-clad figure in the room at the top of the East Tower. "Exactly how is Ceremonial Magic practiced?" I asked.

He started to pace the room. It wasn't really large enough for pacing, so he soon sat down on the window seat.

"There is a belief . . . *was* a belief," he corrected himself, "in the existence of thousands of, shall we say, entities."

"Entities?"

"Spirits. Beings."

"Demons?" I asked.

He smiled. "Some have called them that, yes. Let's stick with 'entities'. These entities exist in a different plane of existence from ours. Yet if you have the formula – know the correct ritual to perform – you can make them appear here. They do not *want* to come; they would far rather not. But if you know the correct Words of Power with which to conjure them, you can make them appear."

"But why would anyone want to do that?" I asked.

"I'm coming to that. You see, each of these entities is responsible for a different thing. One can give you the power to see into the future. Another knows where all hidden treasures are buried. Yet another can teach you healing, or foreign languages, or the secret of invisibility. Now, if you can make one appear then he has to acknowledge you as his master and give you whatever is his specialty."

"I see," I said slowly. It really sounded rather fascinating, if a little like something out of *The Arabian Nights*. "And how do you know which one you want to appear?"

"That's again where the grimoire comes in. In it is listed all the entities, together with their specialties. And it tells you exactly how to conjure each one."

I thought of the time I was in the library and read all those strange titles. I remembered looking at that list of names . . . the one that included Sirdah. Was Sirdah, then, one of these entities and had been conjured here? The thought sent shivers up and down my spine.

"Has anybody ever really done this?" I asked. "I mean, really conjured up one of these beings and then got something?"

"Oh, yes."

"How do you know?"

He smiled. "My ancestor did it. Sir Gilbert Fletcher."

I gasped.

"Yes, good old Sir Gilbert," he continued. "That was how he got the money to build his castle in England, all those centuries ago."

"You mean . . ."

"Yes. He just conjured up the entity in charge of gold, or whatever, and bingo! He was in business."

I thought for a moment. "And what about your grandfather?" I said, slowly. "How did he get his money?"

"Old Henry?" John frowned. "I'm not sure. He certainly got a whole lot of money from somewhere. Yet he ran out of it before he could finish the place."

"Didn't Cynthia once tell me that he threw himself off the top of the East Tower when he couldn't complete it?"

"Oh, yes." He nodded. "And that was strange. From all I've heard, he wasn't the sort to commit suicide, especially over a frustration like that. He'd have been far more likely to have gone and tried to get more money from somewhere, to finish the job. But then, perhaps that's what he did."

"What do you mean?"

"Remember I said that Ceremonial Magic is dangerous? Well, perhaps he tried again and didn't do too well."

"What might have happened?"

"If anything goes wrong in the ritual, then the entity can get the upper hand. It can give you a heart attack, have you break out in leprosy . . . jump off a tower! Or simply drive you crazy." This last he said very bitterly, and I wondered why.

At that moment the door was flung open and Cynthia came in carrying a small tray. She seemed surprised to find John sitting so far away from me.

"I guess you heard me coming," she said, setting down the tray on the bedside table.

John got up and made for the door. "Time I went," he said. Cynthia sniffed.

"Thanks for the talk," I said. "I enjoyed it. Oh, and don't bother about that book. It doesn't sound like great reading after all."

He laughed and went out. Cynthia sniffed again.

"I do hope I didn't interrupt anything," she said. "I just thought you might enjoy a glass of warm milk. Always helps when you're feeling low. Here! Drink it up."

She held the glass in front of me. I don't care too much for milk at the best of times and I really didn't want it then.

"Leave it on the tray, Cynthia," I said. "Thank you for thinking of it, but I'll have it in a little while."

"You really should have it now, you know. While it's hot."

"No. I won't let it get cold but not right this minute."

She hesitated, and then put the glass back down on the tray.

"Well, all right, then. But you promise me you'll drink it?"

"I will, Cynthia," I said. "I promise."

It was really very sweet of her to think of it, I thought. Sometimes she surprised me when she allowed her maternal side to show. She plumped up my pillows and went out, closing the door gently behind her.

I lay quiet for a while, thinking over what John had told me about Ceremonial Magic. I was certain it was just such a ritual that I had witnessed being attempted in the East Tower room. Babula had probably got hold of the grimoire, as John called it, and was trying some magic for his own ends. I wondered if I should tell John about it? But to do so would mean I'd have to admit to going into the forbidden East Tower. I decided to wait awhile and see if anything further developed.

I reached out for the glass of milk; I didn't want to disappoint Cynthia. As I lifted it, the bottom of the glass caught on the rim of the tray and it slipped from my fingers. The glass fell to the floor and, although it didn't break, the milk went flying all over the floor and the bedside rug. I hopped out of bed to get a towel from the bathroom, to mop it up. My foot went right in the milk and I cursed.

As I wiped my foot with the towel, I noticed something strange. Mixed in with the milk was a gritty powder. I examined it closely. It was yellowish and, when I touched it to my tongue, tasted bitter. I decided that Cynthia must have crushed up an aspirin and put it in the milk, yet it didn't really taste like aspirin. A horrible thought came to me . . . could Cynthia be trying to poison me?

Chapter Nineteen

As Cynthia drew closer to finishing her screenplay, I expected her to get happier. But she didn't. If it was possible, she grew more changeable than ever. One minute she would smile at me but the next she would be screaming over some imagined wrong. She more frequently called me Julie, by mistake, and started muttering to herself a great deal. I was very worried and suggested to John that perhaps she should see a doctor.

"Nonsense," he said. "Cynthia is just Cynthia. She has her moments and, as you know, loves to be theatrical. She'll get over whatever is bugging her, you'll see."

Several times in the next few days Peter tried to be along with me. He let me know that there was something important he wanted to discuss. What it could possibly be I had no idea, unless he too was concerned about Cynthia. Anyway, Cynthia watched us like a hawk. You would think she was my chaperone, in Victorian England, on the lookout for undesirable young men who might attempt to take advantage of me. We were never left along for one minute.

One afternoon I was returning to the study after a trip to the library, when I saw Babula coming along the corridor towards me. As we neared one another he paused and obsequiously salaamed me, as was his custom. I nodded to him and we continued on our ways. I was just about to open the door to the study when I realized something I had just seen. In glancing down, I had noticed a splash of yellow paint on one of the sneakers that Babula was wearing! *He was wearing Simon's sneakers!* I spun around but Babula had gone. I determined, then and there, that I would pay another visit to the odious East Tower, and somehow I would get into that locked room containing the old man. There had to be some clue there, to the whereabouts of Simon.

It was another couple of days before I had an opportunity to put my plan into action. I once again slipped away early from the dinner table and went quickly down the passage to the locked door. The only disturbing incident was a brief encounter with Sirdah, as I was about to unlock the door. I became aware of someone watching me and, swinging around, saw the cat sitting at the corner where the passageway turned off to Cynthia's and John's rooms. I pretended to be just trying the door and then turned and went into the kitchen. I spoke briefly to Frau Brüning, complimenting her on the dinner, and then returned to the corridor. It was clear; Sirdah had gone. How ridiculous, I thought, to be suspicious of a cat.

The climb up the tower was exhausting but eventually I stood outside the padlocked room, one floor below the top. I listened at the door but could hear nothing from inside. I tapped on it.

"Simon? Simon?"

No answer. I then beat hard on the door, using my fist. Again, no response. I was wondering what I should do next when I finally heard a noise inside. It sounded like a chair being moved; scraping against the stone floor. I beat on the door again.

"Is anybody there?" I called.

"Who . . . who is that?"

The voice sounded old and feeble; in marked contrast to the vibrant screaming I associated with the room.

"Rebecca," I said. "My name is Rebecca. Rebecca Valentine. Who are you?"

There was silence for a long moment and then: "Who are you?"

"Rebecca Valentine," I repeated. "I'm here to help you."

"Oh! Oh, no! Oh, I don't think they'd like that!"

"Who *are* you?" I persisted.

"No, they wouldn't like that at all. Oh, dear me, no! You'd better go away, young lady."

I didn't know what to do. I hadn't expected that kind of a reaction.

"But you don't understand," I said. "I'm here to try to help you. But I need to know who you are. And how you got there. Does anyone on the mainland know you're here?"

"Julie tried to help. Yes, Julie tried to help. She tried to help. And where is she now? Where is Julie? She tried to help. Can't help. Can't help. They won't like it at all. Oh, dear me, no. They won't like it. Better go away." His voice trailed off and I heard shuffling steps as he moved away from the door.

I tried again. For ten minutes or more I beat on the door, pleaded, asked questions, and promised help. But not another word did he say; not another sound came from inside the room. I sat down on the top of the stairs to think out my next move.

I hadn't reached any decision when I was interrupted in my thinking by a sound below me. I strained to listen. Someone was coming up the stairs. I jumped to my feet, blew out my candle, and went as quickly and carefully as I could across to the stairs continuing up. I then stood, scarcely daring to breathe, halfway up the flight, listening.

I could see the flickering light cast by the newcomer's candle, as they reached the landing. Then I heard a knocking on the door I had just stopped beating on. A voice called out to the old man inside. I gasped when I recognized the voice. It was Peter. What was he doing there? He knocked a number of times but got no response. I had almost decided to go down and show myself to Peter – perhaps join forces? – when he apparently turned away and retreated back down the stairs.

I must go down too, I thought. Get back to my room. But I'd better give Peter time to get well clear. I sat down again on the step and waited. Just about the time I decided to make my move I heard voices, and footsteps again, coming up the tower stairs. Now who? I turned and hurried on up to the top floor and then, to be on the safe side, on out to the roof.

It was beautiful up on the East Tower battlements. A marked change from the last time I had been there, blasted by the wind and the rain, and surrounded by lightning. I looked out over the lake, now faintly lit by the moon yet sufficiently illuminated to show the incredible beauty of the view from that height. I would dearly have loved to be able to go up there in the daylight, with my paint box.

Light shone up from the skylight, illuminating the top of the tower and bathing it in an eery green glow. Whoever had followed Peter up the tower must have entered the Ceremonial Magic room – for so I believed it to be – and be planning a ritual. I crept to the edge of the skylight and looked down. Would it be Babula or Cynthia . . . or John?

For some time the person in the room below stayed out of my range of vision. Then I saw him. Clad once again in the hooded red robes, he started his ritual of lighting the black candles about the magic circle. I watched in fascination. Now that I knew a little of Ceremonial Magic, and its purpose, I wished I could see the enactment more clearly.

I had been watching the figure below me for some considerable time when I became aware of someone watching *me*. Almost before I turned around, I knew what I would see. Two small, red eyes glowed at me from the foot of the parapet to my left. Sirdah!

How had he got through the locked door, I wondered? He crouched there, eyes fixed on me; burning into me. It must be the way the moonlight, or the light from the skylight, is reflected, I thought; the way his eyes seemed to glow and to shine as though lit from within. They held my own eyes, locked, and I felt a strange kind of paralysis creeping over me. I wanted to turn and run, but I couldn't. I couldn't even get up off my knees. I sat, transfixed, seeing Sirdah's eyes seemingly growing bigger and bigger. My mouth felt dry and I could not swallow. I was aware of cold sweat up the length of my spine.

"Julie?"

Whether she intended it or not, Cynthia's voice broke the spell. I swung around and came to my feet. Cynthia was standing in the doorway at the head of the stairs. In her eyes I could see something of the pulsating power I had found in Sirdah's. Yet there was also that vacant stare I had noticed before, when she had called me Julie on previous occasions.

"Cynthia," I said. "I – I can explain . . ."

"No-o-o-o." She spoke in a low voice, drawing out the vowel sound. "No, Julie. You can't explain. You see, I already know. I know all. Sirdah told me. Sirdah tells me everything."

I glanced quickly at the cat. He moved stealthily around to join Cynthia, rubbing himself against her legs yet never taking his eyes off me.

"Cynthia, you don't understand. I'm not Julie."

"I don't know why you came back," she said, not listening to what I told her. "I sent you away once, didn't I? You weren't supposed to come back."

"I'm not Julie," I pleaded. "Please, Cynthia. Listen to me."

"You're not going to take my husband away from me, Julie. Oh, no! You're not going to have him, d'you hear?"

"Cynthia! What – what are you talking about? You're not even married. And even if you were, I would never . . ."

"Silence! I don't want to listen to you, pretty Julie!"

She started towards me and I backed away. I hadn't far to go before I came up against the stone parapet around the top of the tower. She was obviously insane. But what did she mean? There must be some basis for her crazed words, I reasoned. Could it be that she really was married? Perhaps the old man locked in the room below was her husband? Perhaps they had both gone insane! John had locked up the husband, I reasoned, but couldn't bear to do the same to his own sister. Poor John! My heart went out to him.

"Such a pretty face," Cynthia said, as she drew nearer. "So fine, and such an attraction to my love. Poor darling. He is weak, you see. He cannot help himself. Not like me. I am strong! And I have . . . Sirdah!"

The cat leapt up into her arms and she petted him and held him close.

"At least no one can take away Sirdah," she continued. Holding the cat close to her with one hand, she suddenly reached out and grasped the collar of my blouse, which stuck out above my sweater. "Such pretty things you wear, Julie." She fondled the material. "Such pretty things. And all to snare my love! That's wicked, you know? Wicked! And you know what happens to wicked girls, don't you? It happened to you once before, Julie – oh, why did you come back? – and it's going to happen again."

Her eyes grew large and I saw a trickle of saliva at the corner of her mouth. My God, she's going to kill me! I thought.

"Now, Julie! Now!" she screamed and lunged forward.

I tried to duck to one side. I felt a tug at my neck as I fell to my knees and rolled on the floor. I was crying and sobbing as I lay there. Then I realized that all had gone quiet.

With the backs of my hands, I rubbed the tears from my eyes and looked around me. I was alone. I looked to where I had been standing against the parapet and saw that I had been at the point where the built-up section ended. Another foot or two to one side and there was nothing . . . just the edge of the roof.

I crawled to the edge and, lying on my stomach, looked over. Far, far below me, in the weak light of the moon, was what looked like a dark shadow on the rocks. I knew it was no shadow; it was Cynthia. Cynthia still cradling Sirdah. I thought it strange that she had made no sound, emitted no scream, as she fell. But then, who can fathom the minds of the insane?

I rolled over on to my back and lay, for a long time, gathering myself together again. That could have been me, lying broken at the foot of the tower. I had come to Fletcher Island looking for excitement . . . but I hadn't bargained for this! I determined to leave first thing in the morning. Dear, safe Boston looked like paradise to me now. Never again would I complain about the drudgery of typing, filing, and dictation. I would have given anything to be back in my old apartment right then and there.

I started to shiver. I don't know if it was the cold, up there on the top of the tower, or a delayed shock reaction. Probably a little of both. I got up, went over to the stairs, and started down them. At the door to the top room I paused and listened. The perfume of incense seeped out and surrounded me. It was not a pleasant incense; it had a sweet and sickly odor that almost made me gag. I covered my mouth and nose with my handkerchief and listened.

There was no chanting but I could hear the footsteps of the magician as he moved about his circle. It suddenly struck me that perhaps he was finishing up his work and tidying up before leaving the room. The thought of another encounter with anyone, after what I had just gone through, made me move hurriedly away from the door and feel my way down the stairs.

Passing the old man's door, I paused long enough to light my candle and then continued descending the tower steps. No sound came from the old man's room and I was certainly not going to try any further communication that night. I did wonder if the prisoner was really Cynthia's husband. His voice had sounded old; much older than her. Yet I had long since discovered that you can't go by voices. Besides, he might well have been older than her anyway. Why not?

I reached the bottom of the tower and listened briefly at the door of the Fletchers' apartment for sounds of John. All was quiet. All at once I realized that I couldn't tell him, or anyone, of Cynthia's death! If I did, then I would have to explain what I was doing up in the East Tower in the first place. How could I admit to spying and prying when John had expressly forbidden me to enter the tower? Yet I had to let him know that his sister was dead. Should I go out early in the morning and act as though I had just happened upon the body? I could never do that, I thought. And besides, why would I have "just happened" to be all the way over by the East Tower? No, I would have to think of something else. Perhaps I could be taking flowers to place on the spot where poor Sara had fallen?

I continued on to my room, my head spinning. I had to get some rest and then consider it in the morning. But then another thought struck me. Wouldn't John miss his sister when she didn't appear in their rooms that night? Which brought me to a question that had been nagging at the back of my mind for a long time . . . why was there only one bed in the Fletchers' apartment? It worried me. And now – if in fact they *did* sleep together – John would be certain to miss Cynthia tonight. In fact, he might even now be looking for her.

At last, thankfully, I came to my room. How I looked forward to climbing into bed, closing my eyes, and my mind, to the whole ugly, confusing mess. I needed to sleep. I put out my hand . . . and found that the door was already open.

Chapter Twenty

"Good heavens! You look terrible!" Peter was sitting on the chest at the foot of my bed. He came to his feet as I entered the room, and hurried over to me. "What on earth happened to you? Here, come and sit down."

He led me to the bed and I thankfully sank down onto it and lay back. Peter went across, closed the bedroom door, and locked it. He then came and sat on the edge of the bed beside me.

"Tell me about it," he said, his voice soft and gentle. "But only if you feel up to it."

"I'm all right . . . now," I said. I looked up at him. His big, brown eyes showed genuine concern and his knit brow made me want to reassure him. "Honestly. I'm okay."

He smiled. I thought how attractive he was when he smiled. Why had I taken a dislike to him before? Though it hadn't really been a dislike; more of a wariness. Now, those thin lips and sharp features I had before viewed with suspicion looked intelligent and comforting. A lock of his black hair fell forward over his forehead, adding to the attraction I was finding in this close scrutiny. I smiled back at him.

"That's better," he said. "Now just relax and get yourself back together. Then, when you feel ready, tell me what you've been up to."

I closed my eyes for a moment and breathed deeply. I really was beginning to feel better.

"What happened to your blouse?" Peter asked. "The collar has been ripped right off."

I put up my hand and felt the ragged edge. A vision of Cynthia grasping the collar, and the sharp tug I felt as she lunged at me, brought back full memory of the nightmare on the tower. I suddenly burst into a flood of tears.

"Becky!"

Peter's arm was around me in a flash. I let myself be pulled to his chest and encircled by his arms. I sobbed my heart out on his sweater while he cradled me, smoothing my hair, and kissing the top of my head.

"Becky! Becky! There! That's it. Get it out. Let yourself go."

The tears were certainly a relief. It was like opening a valve in order to lower pressure. All of the uneasiness, the suspicions, the terrors of the past weeks came together and burst out, leaving me drained but feeling much, much better. And leaving Peter with a sodden sweater! I started to apologize, as I recovered and – not without reluctance – pushed myself away from him again.

"Don't be silly. You're welcome to wet my sweater any time you want. Feeling better now?"

I nodded and, reaching for my handkerchief, blew my nose.

"Feel like talking about it? Talking helps too, you know?"

I nodded again. "Yes, you're right." I looked at him, though I realized I must have red, swollen eyes, and must look a sight. He didn't seem to notice. "Cynthia's dead," I said.

Peter's mouth set a little grimly, but he said nothing.

"She fell from the tower . . . the East Tower. She was trying to push me over the edge of it."

"Trying to . . . oh, my god! No wonder you're in such a state."

He took me in his arms again and held me tightly. I didn't protest. I was coming to enjoy the feeling of protection, and tenderness. I told him what had happened. I went right back to the beginning, to my arrival with Simon. I told him of Simon's disappearance and of finding his windbreaker in the room up on the third floor. Also of Babula apparently wearing Simon's sneakers.

When I mentioned the other clothes I had found – Julie's – and of Cynthia repeatedly calling me Julie, he became very interested.

"The blouse. The yellow blouse. Do you have it here?"

"Yes," I said. "It's hanging in the wardrobe over there."

He went over and took it out. He stood for a long time, holding it and staring at it.

"What's the matter, Peter? Did you know the girl?"

He put back the blouse and then came and sat beside me again. "Yes. Yes, I knew her. She worked in my office for a while."

"In your office?" I didn't understand. "She was with the movie company?"

"No," he said. "I don't work for a movie company. The closest I ever got to actors was a short stint with a local repertory company just after college, as a break before going into law. I work for a law firm."

My mind went back to an earlier discovery. I dug into the back pocket of my jeans and pulled out the now crumpled business card I had been carrying around for the better part of a week or more.

"Phelps, Cotterell, Bryant, and Martine," I read. "And you are an Associate."

Peter's face blanched. "Where did you get that?"

I laughed, and told him about knocking over his briefcase.

He grimaced. "Lucky for me it was you who found it," he said. "Very sloppy of me. Could have blown the whole thing."

"What whole thing? What's going on, Peter?"

He smiled. "You finish telling me your story and then I'll tell you mine."

It didn't take long to finish telling mine. And since I was eager to find out more about Peter Southwood, and his reasons for being there at Fletcher's Folly, I hurried through it.

"First of all," he said, when it was his turn. "I'm afraid we must figure on Simon being dead."

"Oh, no!"

"From what you say, I'm willing to bet that what you saw from Simon's window, that first night, was Babula dumping the body in the lake. Weighted with cement, of course."

Deep down inside I must have known that Simon was dead, and been prepared for the news. It numbed me only slightly, after the deaths of Sara and Cynthia.

"But why would anyone kill Simon?" I asked. "He'd done nothing to anyone. All he did was give me a lift over here."

"That's it, you see. *He knew you were here.* They didn't want *anyone* to know you were here. Didn't you say the original plan was for them to pick you up in Meredith?"

I nodded.

"There, then. And who would think of leaving from Meredith to come all the way out to Fletcher Island?"

"But what about the captain of the sightseeing boat?" I asked. "He brought me most of the way, so he knew I was here."

"Captain? What sightseeing boat? Didn't Simon bring you all the way, then?"

"No," I said. "Only from Egypt Island, where the captain dropped me off. Red was his name, or Rusty, or something like that."

"Did John and Cynthia know this?"

I thought for a moment. "No. I guess they didn't. There'd be no reason for them to. I guess they just assumed that Simon brought me all the way, as you did."

Peter was quiet for a moment, deep in thought.

"You keep speaking of 'they'," I said. "Just who do you mean by 'they'? Isn't Babula the bad guy?"

He shook his head. I noticed, for the first time, that he looked very, very tired. "No," he said. "Babula is only an instrument."

"But . . . isn't it he who is working Ceremonial Magic in that room at the top of the East Tower?"

"Good heavens, no! Babula hasn't the power, or the authority, to do that. No. That Master Magician is none other than friend John Fletcher."

"John?" I was aghast. " *John*, you say?"

I thought of John and the last time he had touched me. It had been right here, in my bedroom, when I was recovering from my cold. He had held my hand between his and seemed so concerned for me. No! Peter must be mistaken, I thought. Then I remembered John's warning, when Peter had first arrived at Fletcher's Folly: "I wouldn't place too much trust in that Southwood if I were you." I looked across at Peter. He must have known what was in my mind.

"Warned you against me, didn't he?"

I nodded. He smiled grimly.

"Guessed as much. Look, Becky. Who told you all about this Ceremonial Magic in the first place?"

"Why, John did."

"Uhu! And who owns the books of magic you saw in the library?"

"Well, John . . . or Cynthia, I guess."

"Right. But Cynthia was busy trying to push you off the tower while the magician was at work, wasn't she?"

I nodded. He was right. It had to be John in the magic room, just as it had to be John behind Simon's death. I had a sudden thought.

"Who is the old man locked in the tower, Peter?"

"I don't know." He shook his head.

"Is it Cynthia's husband? When she was trying to kill me, thinking I was Julie, she kept saying that I was trying to steal her husband. I didn't even know she was married."

"Well, she is. But not to the old man in the tower . . . whoever he is. No." He looked at me, his eyes searching my face. "She's married to John, Becky. They're husband and wife."

He couldn't have startled me more if he had tried. But of course! It all made sense now. It explained the one double bed in their apartment, and the arguments I had caught snatches of.

"But why?" I asked. "Why would John be so . . ." I blushed and lowered my eyes. "Why would they pretend to be brother and sister?"

Peter stood up and stretched.

"For very good reasons," he said, cryptically. "But I'm afraid the rest of the story will have to wait."

"Why? What do you mean?"

He leaned close and took my hands in both of his.

"Cynthia's death is going to precipitate things. I can't – I daren't – stop to explain everything now. When I come back I will."

"Come back? Where are you going?"

He caught the rising hysteria in my voice and squeezed my hands. "You'll be all right. I'm going to have to get to the mainland and get some action going. Don't worry. John won't let anything happen to you . . . yet. But with Cynthia dead he's going to move ahead with his plans, if I know him. Don't worry, Becky. I'll be back here before you know it, and everything will be over."

He bent and kissed me softly on the lips. My heart skipped several beats and I must have dug my nails into his hands as I gripped them. He didn't flinch. I had no idea of the meaning of half of what Peter had said, but I heard him say he'd be back before I knew it. Yes, I thought, I do trust Peter Southwood.

He let go my hands, stood up, and tugged on his left ear in his nervous habit. I knew from that, that he was worried.

"I'll have to sneak off right away," he said, half to himself. "John's probably prowling around, looking for Cynthia. That's if he's finished his devilish ritual."

He looked at me again and smiled. "Be brave, Becky. You'll be all right."

Peter turned and went out, quietly closing the door behind him.

Chapter Twenty-One

I had never seen John so angry. He did not seem concerned about Cynthia's disappearance. He seemed to think that she had simply got up early and gone out. By that, I presumed that he had not returned from his magical exploits in the tower until the early hours of the morning. But he was seething with anger that Peter had gone.

"His bed was not slept in," he said, pacing up and down the sitting room. "His things are gone. He has obviously left the island."

"But – but, how?" I asked.

"In *my boat!*" he thundered.

I pulled back in my chair.

"I'm sorry, Rebecca," he said. "I shouldn't take out my anger on you. It's just that Cynthia's precious Mr. Southwood has seen fit to abscond with my boat."

"But I thought he had his own boat," I said.

"Seems there was something wrong with the engine. I guess he couldn't get it started. Babula is down at the boathouse now, trying to fix it. Then I can go after him."

"Are you sure he's gone for good?" I asked, as innocently as I could. "Perhaps he just had to go to the mainland to get something."

"Then why did he take all of his clothes with him?"

I hung my head.

"I also gave him strict instructions that if he ever needed anything I would send Babula across for him."

"Cynthia had finished the screenplay, you know," I said.

"I know! That's probably it. The ingrate just grabbed it up and took off. No thought of saying 'thank you,' for putting up with him all this time! Too damned anxious to get back to his movie offices. Didn't I tell you not to trust him? Didn't I?"

"Yes," I said. "You did, John."

He paced up and down for a while longer, then stopped.

"Wait! I bet this was Cynthia's idea. I bet *she* sent him off in such a hurry. She can't wait to see her name up on that big screen. Where the devil is she?"

"I – I haven't seen her since . . ." I gulped. "Since dinner last night."

"Hmm. Think I'll go and look for her." Still bristling, he left the room.

It was lunchtime before they found the body. Babula, after having got the outboard engine running again, joined John in combing the island for Cynthia.

I couldn't bear to join them, as John suggested, swearing off with a headache. When they carried her in I was surprised to find John seemingly as little affected by it as he had been by Sara's death.

"Where did you find her?" I asked.

"At the foot of the East Tower," he said. "Seems to have become the center-point of the island." He brushed some dirt from the knees of his tailored pants.

"W-Was it an accident, do you think?" I asked, my voice quavering.

"Either that or suicide," he responded. "What she was doing up on top of the tower, I don't know. We went up . . ." He turned away from me. "Had to go up, to check a room up there late yesterday evening. But I thought she came straight down again."

He poured himself a whiskey and knocked it back. Perhaps he was affected after all, I thought.

Suddenly John swung around, his eyes blazing. I gripped the arms of my chair.

"That's it!" he cried. "Why didn't I put two and two together before? Southwood killed her! Why else would he have gone running off like that? He pushed her off the tower!"

"Oh, no!" I jumped to my feet. "No, you're wrong. He couldn't . . ."

"Couldn't? What do you mean? Why not? What do you know, Rebecca?"

I gulped. I was in a dilemma. How could I draw suspicion away from Peter and not involve myself?

"It's just . . . no! He *liked* Cynthia. Why would he kill her? What possible motive would he have had?"

"I don't know. I just don't know." John was quieting down again.

I had an idea. "We had better contact the police," I said.

"No!"

I rather thought – and hoped- that would be his reaction.

"No! Not until I've got this whole thing clearer in my head. No! No, we don't want to go accusing anyone without proof. No sense in jumping to conclusions and then having dozens of policemen swarming all over the island, and the castle."

He ran his fingers through his hair, his forehead furrowed, the eyebrows drawn tightly together. I could see he was working on what best to do. He obviously had no wish to bring the authorities to Fletcher Island, especially if Peter and I had been right in our guesses concerning Simon and Julie.

John took another drink. "I'll go and see how Frau Brüning is doing," he said. "She's laying out the body."

After he had left the room I went out of the castle and down to the dock. Peter had said that I wasn't to worry; that no harm could come to me. Yet I was frightened. I was alone on the island with two men, one of whom was a murderer, and Frau Brüning. The cook had shown some friendliness, in her own way, during the time I had been at Fletcher's Folly. Hadn't she even once warned me to get away from there? . . . Oh, why hadn't I listened, I thought? I should have gone . . . But I couldn't count on Frau Brüning. After all, she had been on the island for years; had been with the Fletchers a lifetime. No, it was obvious where her loyalties would lie.

I looked at the outboard, tied-up to the dock where Babula had been working on it. It was fixed now and ready to go. It would be so easy to jump down into it, start it up, and get away from there. I was tempted; sorely tempted.

"Don't try it, Rebecca."

I jumped, and turned to see John scowling down at me.

"I – that is – don't do what, John?" I tried to sound innocent.

"I know what was going through your mind," he said. His voice was harsh. His eyes – oh, how they reminded me of Sirdah's – were sunken in their sockets, yet they seemed to glow. He suddenly looked older. The light was behind him and made the periphery of his hair appear almost white. His cheeks seemed to have sunken in; his face was lined. He held out his closed hand to me, and then opened it. Across his palm lay the torn collar of my blouse.

"You don't seem to understand," I said. "Cynthia was trying to kill me. She thought I was Julie. She kept calling me 'Julie'. She said I was trying to steal her husband."

At that, John turned to face me.

We were back in the sitting room. I was sitting in one of the armchairs – the one Cynthia had always sat in – and John was interrogating me. That was the only word for it: interrogating. Instead of being the one who had been attacked, I was being treated like the attacker.

"Your blouse collar was found clutched in Cynthia's hand."

"I've told you, she grabbed me and tore it as she fell."

John poured himself a whiskey. I had never known him to drink so much. It frightened me.

"You were spying. You know you had no business in the East Tower. Why did you go there, despite my forbidding it?"

I sighed. "I already told you," I said. "I saw someone at the window, near the top, when I was out in the garden. I wanted to find out who it was." I paused, then: "I thought that perhaps the old man was Cynthia's husband."

"What?" John spun around and, to my amazement, burst out laughing. "Oh, no," he said. "No. He's not her husband."

"I know that now," I said.

"Why, Cynthia wasn't even married."

"Oh yes she was," I said. "To you."

The smile froze on his face, and then gave way to a smirk. "So you know that, do you?"

"Yes."

"And how did you find out, might I ask?"

"Peter . . ."

"Southwood? My! Our absconding friend left no stone unturned, did he?"

"But why did you have to pretend you weren't married?" I asked.

"You'll find that out soon enough. Soon enough. Come! I want you to meet someone." He put down his glass, seized my hand, and led my brusquely from the room.

We went through the door at the end of the passageway. Apparently it was now unlocked, and we were going to the East Tower.

"You must know the way pretty well by now," said John, still holding my arm.

We climbed up to the first of the locked doors; the room where the old man lived. John took out a key and undid the padlock. I didn't know what to expect. Was he going to lock me in there as well? Was I going to be a cellmate to the demented old man who screamed so pitifully every night? I hung back but John took my arm again and marched me into the room.

It was barely furnished. There was a small wooden table and one chair, a chest of drawers, and what looked to be an old army cot. There were no rugs on the floor and in one corner was an open toilet and enclosed shower stall. I looked around in disgust. No priceless antiques here. The old man lay on the cot.

"This," said John, indicating the sleeping figure, " is my father."

Chapter Twenty-Two

I could see the resemblance. The old man must have been tall when he stood up. Perhaps even taller than his son. He had the same sensuous, thick lips; the same eagle's beak of a nose; and, I suspected, the same hypnotic eyes. His hair was gray, turning to white.

"Your father?" I said. "And you keep him here, locked up?"

John walked over to the sleeping figure and looked down on him.

"Either locked up here or locked away in some terrible asylum with people who don't care whether he lives or dies." He turned to face me. "He's mad, you see. Absolutely, completely insane."

I was beginning to have doubts about the son's sanity, but I dare not say so. I looked about me, at the crude, bare furnishings.

"I know what you're thinking," said John. "But really, it doesn't make any difference to him how elaborate or how simple are his surroundings. It's the . . . the care, that matters."

I walked over to the window and looked down. I could see the dock and the boathouse, off to the right, and a little of the front lawn. I looked out over the waters of the lake, to the peaks of the White Mountains in the distance. If the view could make up for anything, the old man had the best. I ran my hands over the bars at the window. They looked new.

"I had to put those on," said John. "I didn't want to but, after what happened to Sara . . ."

"What do you mean?" I swung around.

John bit his lip. "She didn't get blown off the top of the tower," he said, his voice low. "She used to bring my father his food. One night she caught him at a bad time . . . He threw her from the window." His voice shook a little. "Never been violent before."

He turned his back to me and, for a moment, I felt like running to him, to comfort him. But then I thought of Simon, and of Julie.

"How did he get this way, John?" I asked.

"Magic."

"What?"

"Magic. Ceremonial Magic." He was himself again and started pacing the room. "I told you, if you remember, that it had claimed many victims. My father is one of them, though he wasn't so lucky. He is still alive!"

"What do you mean?"

"He would have been better off dead!" He stopped pacing and perched himself on the edge of the table. I moved the chair out and sat down.

"How did it happen?" I asked. "What was he trying to do?"

"Do? Why, to raise the money to finish grandfather's castle, of course. But . . . something went wrong."

"And is that what you're trying to do; in that room above this one?"

He looked at me, one eyebrow raised. "Your spying is thorough," he said. "Yes. I *was* going to follow the route of the Fletchers before me. I do keep my hand in, with various of the simpler, and less dangerous, rituals, from time to time." He stood up. "But now that I have you, I don't have to risk my life . . ." He glanced at the figure still sleeping on the cot. "Or my sanity. It's safe."

"I don't understand. What have I got to do with it?"

John took me back down to the main house. We went to the study and there he sat me down at the table. The table where I had worked for so long, it seemed, with his wife Cynthia. She had been mad too, I thought. Was there a curse on the family? I could certainly believe there was.

John ferreted in the drawer of Cynthia's roll-top desk, and then emptied the contents on to the table. I heard a slight *click* and watched him remove a false bottom from the drawer. He pulled out a document that had lain hidden there.

"Here!" he said, putting it down in front of me. "Sign that."

I looked. It was a will.

"But . . . what . . . ?"

"Just sign it," he said.

"No!" I was suddenly frightened. "Not without an explanation."

"All right. You can read it."

I did. It seemed to be a straightforward will, so far as I could see. It was already made out in my name, and it left everything I had – how little *that* was, I thought! – to . . . my husband!

"I don't get it," I said. "I have nothing worth leaving anyone, and I have no husband."

"Wrong. Now sign it."

He was mad, I decided. Completely and utterly insane.

"No." I was firm. "I won't sign it."

John put his hand in his pocket and slowly drew out the torn collar of my blouse; the one Cynthia had ripped from me.

"If you don't sign," he said, "I'm afraid I shall have to charge you with Cynthia's murder. And you know I don't want to do that."

Humor him, I thought. Humor him. What harm would there be in signing? Anything to keep him happy till Peter got back. I signed.

"That's a sensible girl."

"But it's ridiculous," I said. "I'm not married."

"No. But you're going to be."

My heart sank. He took the paper and locked it away again in the desk drawer. Then he took me up to my room and stood at the door looking at me.

"You're going to make me a beautiful bride, Rebecca. I can see that. No, don't say anything! Just listen. I'd planned to marry you all along. Cynthia wasn't too thrilled with the idea, I must admit. Can't think why. Anyway, now she's taken care of. I must thank you for that. She was always a jealous woman, anyway. Even when I had that harmless little flirtation with Julie. Cynthia couldn't stand it. Well, she got her just desserts. But now I'm truly free and we are to be married. I'm sending Babula to the mainland right away, to get a Justice of the Peace to perform the ceremony and take care of the paperwork. Frau Brüning will be up later to fit you for your wedding dress. It will be the traditional Fletcher one. My mother was married in it, and my grandmother. And, of course, Cynthia."

My blood ran cold. He was obviously quite mad.

"I would not advise you to attempt to leave your room. You will note, I have had Babula fix a large new padlock on the outside of your door. I think you will be secure."

"But why? Why do you want to marry me?" I asked.

"Don't you know?" he said. "You're an heiress."

Chapter Twenty-Three

It didn't make sense. Whichever way I looked at it, it didn't make any sense. I was an orphan, not an heiress. I had spent my childhood being shuffled from orphanage to foster home, and back again. Why, I had moved so much I didn't even know where I had started!

Perhaps that was it, I thought. I *didn't* know where I had started. My beginnings, to all intents and purposes, were when I was saved from an orphanage fire. All records of my origins had been destroyed. Did John know something I didn't? If so, how? How had he found out? *Was* I an heiress? It all came back to the same thing . . . it made absolutely no sense!

One thing that was certain was that I had to get away. There was no way I was going to be married to such a madman. One time, I thought bitterly, I would have jumped at the chance of marrying John. My thoughts went back to the times he and I had spent together in the grounds in front of the castle. Times we had spent just sitting, gazing out over the water or strolling through the trees, laughing at the squirrels and chipmunks, the robins and the bluebirds. I thought of the time when he had almost kissed me, as we stood foolishly balanced on the top of a huge boulder, admiring the castle.

The castle! My prison. The bitterness returned. All those times, all those moments I had thought so precious, he had been making a fool out of me. He was married. And, worse, his wife was aiding and abetting his masquerade. I hurled a pillow across the room, from where I sat on the bed.

I knew I had to escape. Peter would come for me, I knew. Dear Peter. How I had misjudged him in the beginning. I only hoped that *he* didn't turn out to be married! But I couldn't just sit there and wait. What if Peter didn't come in time to save me from the impending wedding ceremony? What if he hadn't made it to the mainland safely? Although the weather had changed for the better, and the waters calmed considerably, there were still a lot of white caps in evidence. And he had left in the antique boat of John's. What if this had sprung a leak, or something?

I went to the window and looked out. There was no sign of any boat drifting about in the distance. I knew there wouldn't be. I was getting silly, I told myself.

The sun was going down I wondered if John had yet sent Babula for the Justice of the Peace. If so, they wouldn't be back until the morning. At least I had twelve hours or so to get myself out of the mess I was in. I looked down at the trees and bushes and sparse grass below the window. Perhaps I could escape that way, I thought? I was only on the second floor. But how would I get down? Knotted bed-sheets was the approved method, I understood. I went back to the bed and threw myself down on it. Climbing down knotted sheets from my bedroom window . . . what an idea! But it just might come to that.

For some reason I thought of the secret drawer John had opened in Cynthia's desk. Old man Fletcher, John's grandfather, seemed to have faithfully followed the construction details of the old European castles, when he built Fletcher's Folly. Could he have done for the castle what was done for that desk drawer? Could he have built-in one or two secret passages, with hidden entrances . . . sliding panels? It was possible, I told myself. Lots of European castles had them. At least, they always showed them in late night movies on television. It might be worth a try.

I got up off the bed and started going, systematically, around the room. I tapped on the paneling, listening for hollow spots; I twisted and pressed every carved wooden knob and ornamentation I could find. No luck. Grandfather Fletcher had no imagination, I decided! The only answer seemed to be the window. But I would have to wait till it was dark.

I bathed, brushed my teeth and hair, and climbed into bed. I set my little alarm clock for two o'clock in the morning and lay down to get some rest. Sleep did not come easily. Small wonder, I thought, considering what I had been through in the previous twenty-four hours. I tossed and turned fitfully but finally dozed off. It was not a good sleep. I seldom remember my dreams but that night they stood out vividly. I may never forget them.

I dreamed of bring chased up and down the East Tower by Cynthia and Sirdah. Just when I thought I had given one of them the slip, I came face to face with the other one. I finally rushed up to the top of the tower, where I found John waiting for me. He said he would save me. All I had to do was put on his mother's wedding dress and jump from the tower. Babula would catch me at the bottom, he said. As I stood in a quandary, all four of them – John, Cynthia, Babula, and Sirdah – rushed at me and pushed me over the edge. I fell, screaming, and woke up soaked in sweat.

I looked at the clock. It was almost one-thirty. Close enough, I thought. I got up and dressed in jeans, my thickest sweater, and sneakers. I dragged the sheets and blankets off the bed and ripped them lengthwise into long strips. These I tied end to end, breaking my nails in the process. I tied one end of this ungainly rope to the bottom post of the bed and, opening the window, dropped the rest over the sill.

I leaned over and looked down. It was almost a new moon – in the fourth quarter – and there was not much light, but I could see that my escape line was short by quite a few feet. I drew it back up and looked around. The only things left were the drapes of the window, the towels, and the shower curtain. I didn't bother with the towels . . . by the time they had been knotted there wouldn't have been much useful length added. The rest, I added to the rope and said a short prayer.

Climbing down was easy. With all the knots, I had plenty to hold on to without fear of slipping. I reached the end and prepared to drop the last couple of feet. I looked down to check my landing area. It was a good thing I did. By the faint light of the moon, directly below me I caught the glint of metal teeth. One of the bear traps! John had actually placed a bear trap under my window just in case I decided to climb out. My bitterness towards him doubled.

I could not climb up the rope again. Even if I had the desire, I did not have the strength. Putting my feet against the rough stones of the castle wall, I "walked" myself backwards and forwards until I'd generated a considerable swing on my rope. Then, choosing my moment carefully, I let go and swung out to land a few feet to one side of the trap. I was shaken by the drop, but not hurt. I ran into the darkness of the trees.

The next half hour was a nightmare in itself. I had to work my way around to the front of the castle and the boathouse. I dared not go too far into the trees in case I got lost in the darkness, yet I dared not stay too close to the castle either. All the time, as I felt my way forward, I had to search the ground for hidden bear traps. John certainly had a penchant for them and, I had to admit, they were very effective.

Finally, weary and disheveled, I came out on the front lawn above the dock. I paused, listening carefully. A bat zigzagged around me and I beat at it with my hands. All was quiet but for the croaking of some frogs and the occasional distant hoot of an owl. I followed around the edge of the trees, down to the water and then ran swiftly across to the boathouse.

The door creaked as I eased it open, but I was sure no one could hear it. Inside it was almost pitch black. It took some time for my eyes to adjust but eventually I was able to make out dark shapes. It was then that the awful truth dawned on me.

John unlocked the padlock and led the way into my room. He went across to the window and pulled in my makeshift rope.

"I'll leave you to untangle the bedclothes," he said.

I glumly took them from him and, sitting down on the bed, started tugging at the knots.

"You can still catch a few hours sleep," he said. "Thanks to your alarm clock."

"What do you mean?" I looked up at him.

"Well, Rebecca, I was just checking on your door before retiring when I became aware of your alarm clock ringing its heart out. I felt sure you couldn't be sleeping through a racket like that, so I came in to investigate."

"And found me gone."

"Precisely. Very ingenious, and I congratulate you. But why did you leave the clock to ring?"

"I woke before it went off," I said. "And forgot to reset it."

"Not that it would have made any difference to the outcome of your attempted escape."

"No," I said. "I realized that, down at the boathouse. There's no boat here, is there? Babula took the outboard to go and get the Justice."

"An island is really the ideal prison," said John, smugly. "Even Napoleon found that. Of course, you could have tried to swim for it."

"You know I couldn't. The closest other island is Egypt and that's much too far to swim."

"Ah! You know your lake, I see." He went to the door. "I don't think I even need to lock the padlock now, do I? Sleep well, my pet."

He went out and closed the door behind him. I fell forward, on the stretched and knotted bedding, and burst into tears.

I did manage to sleep for a few hours but was hard put to rouse myself when Frau Brüning brought in my breakfast tray.

"Good morning." I said, rubbing my eyes.

She was more taciturn than usual and said nothing.

"Is this the morning of my execution?" I asked.

"There is no cause to be joking, Fraulein Rebecca," she said severely. "You should have listened to your betters long since."

By "my betters" I presumed she meant herself. Well, she was right in that I should have listened.

"Has Babula returned yet, with the Justice of the Peace?" I asked.

"*Nein*. There will be plenty of time for me to fix your gown. I shall return in an hour."

She left and, determined to keep up my strength, I ate my breakfast. I was hungrier than I had thought and remembered that I'd had no dinner the previous evening. I showered; partially dressed; and threw on a robe. Where was Peter, I kept thinking? Would he be back in time? If not, and I was forced to go through with the wedding, would the ceremony be valid? Was a wedding vow legal when extracted under duress? I thought not, but then I thought of so-called "shotgun weddings". By all accounts there had been plenty of those in the past, and so far as I knew they had stood up. Then another thought struck me, more terrible by far than any forced marriage.

John had made me sign a will. What he thought I owned, I didn't know. But whatever it was, he intended to inherit it from me. And the only way he could inherit . . . was by my death!

I paced nervously up and down until Frau Brüning returned with the wedding dress. It was truly a beautiful dress that, under different circumstances, I would have adored. Of white silk, it had a high, lace-trimmed collar with a line of tiny, globular, pearl buttons down the front. The mutton-chop sleeves were trimmed with delicate lace, and a lace overskirt covered the voluminous skirt and train. There was little that had to be altered to make it fit me. The hem of the skirt had to be turned up slightly, as did the sleeves, but the waist was a perfect fit. Cynthia, for all her faults, must have looked beautiful on her wedding day, I thought.

"Very nice, Rebecca."

I looked up to see John standing in the doorway. He was wearing the striped pants and gray vest of a mourning suit, though he did not yet have on the tailed coat. He was adjusting his gold cufflinks and a diamond pin in his shirt-front winked in the early morning light.

"I thought prospective bridegrooms were not supposed to see the bride on the wedding day until the actual ceremony," I snapped.

"You are correct." He bowed in deference. "However, I think you will agree that this is a, shall we say, *different* sort of wedding."

"Don't I know it!" I muttered.

"Hold still, if you please." Frau Brüning pulled me roughly around, to stand up straight.

"I thought you would be pleased to know," said John, "that Colonel Sumner, the Justice of the Peace, has just arrived."

My heart sank.

Chapter Twenty-Four

The colonel was an old man; white haired, with a white mustache and bushy eyebrows. He was bent over with age and made a number of complaints that his back bothered him. He shuffled across the sitting room rug to greet me, taking my hands in his and squeezing them. I did not pay too much attention to his mumbled words of greeting and congratulation, since my eyes were beginning to tear and there was a lump developing in my throat.

I was surprised to learn that the Justice had come across to the island alone, piloting himself. I would never have thought him capable of handling a boat at his age and obvious infirmity.

"Been running around all over this lake since I was a kid," he snorted when John commented on it. "No reason to stop now, is there?"

"Then I don't understand about Babula," john said. "He was supposed to bring you back."

"Darn fool foreigner!" The colonel had obviously not taken well to Babula. "Said he had some errand to do in town. Told him I wouldn't wait. My time is precious, even if his isn't. Told him if he weren't back in ten minutes I'd be off. Blame fool! He'll be along sometime, I reckon."

"Well, we're not going to wait for him either," said John. He turned to me. "You look enchanting, my dear. You deserve a suitable setting for this momentous occasion. Let me see, now." He wrinkled his brow in thought. "The Great Banquet Hall? No. It hasn't been used in an age. Too bad I didn't think of that before. I would have had it cleaned."

"I don't mind waiting," I said.

He smiled. "Thank you, Rebecca, but no. Ah! I have it. We will be married in my Ceremonial Magic room in the East Tower. I think that will somehow be appropriate."

"Oh, no!" My heart sank even farther. If the ceremony took place there it would be that much more difficult for Peter to reach me when he arrived.

"The East Tower?" The colonel frowned. "Sounds as though that could involve stairs. I'm not too good with stairs, y'know."

"Don't worry," said John. "I'll help you. You'll be all right."

John led the way down the corridor. The old Justice shuffled after him and I, reluctantly, brought up the rear carrying a candelabra to light our way up the tower stairs. My mind was racing, trying to think of ways to delay us. Perhaps I should pretend to slip on the stairs and twist my ankle? But I quickly realized that wouldn't help. John would insist on carrying me and I couldn't now bear the thought of him touching me.

"Who is going to give me away?" I asked, as we started up the wide, stone steps. "I should have someone to give me away, you know?"

"Indeed you should," agreed John, ahead of me. He had a hand under the colonel's arm and was helping him up the stairs. We made slow progress. "I had thought of that myself and I have come up with an answer . . . the ideal person."

"Frau Brüning?" I couldn't think of anyone else.

"Oh, no! No. She is far too busy preparing our wedding supper."

"Not Babula!" I said. "I refuse to be given away by that . . . . that murderer!"

John paused and looked back at me.

"My!" he said. "You really have the complete picture, haven't you? No, don't worry; I wasn't thinking of Babula. Someone much more appropriate."

"Appropriate?"

"Yes."

Who could he mean, I wondered?

We had reached a landing and paused for the colonel to catch his breath. When we started off again, John signaled for me to go ahead of them.

"A bride should be given away by a father," he said.

"But I – I have no father."

"No." He savored the moment. "But I have."

I stopped in my tracks. My heart pounded against my rib cage. Sweat broke out on my forehead and I dug my nails into the palms of my hands to control myself.

"*Your* father? But he's . . . he's . . ."

"Mad. You can say it, Rebecca. He's mad." He urged me on. "That's all right. He's generally very docile . . . unless excited. He'll be thrilled to handle the bride; you'll see."

We came up to the padlocked door of old William Fletcher, John's father. He must have heard us coming, for he began beating on the door and calling "John! John!"

"Coming, father."

John undid the lock and threw open the door. The old man seemed startled to see so many people there. He had been crying and tears stained his cheeks. He stepped back a pace and his hands began to shake.

"Come, father." John reached out and drew the old man out on to the landing. He was obviously terrified and kept looking about him, is eyes wide.

"Come along," John continued. "We are going to have a wedding and you are going to give away the bride."

His eyes fell on me and, for a moment, they softened. His eyes were like his son's: gray and large. But they had a vacant quality where John's were hypnotic. He seemed troubled as he looked at me. His eyes would move over the wedding dress but when they came back to my face he looked puzzled.

"Cynthia?" he said.

"No, father," said John. "It's not Cynthia. Forget about Cynthia. This is Rebecca."

"'Becca?" he mumbled.

"Come along."

With his father on one side and the colonel on the other, John shepherded us up the last flight of stairs to the Magic Room.

When we went in, I was surprised at the size of the room. It occupied the whole of the top floor of the tower. Rich, red, velvet drapes covered the stone wall and half the huge picture window. John strode across and pulled them back, allowing the sunlight to stream into the room. I set the candelabra down on the floor and blew out its candles.

The floor, as I had seen through the skylight overhead, was decorated with an elaborate magical design. There were three concentric circles, as I had thought, with strange words written between the lines. Some of them I recognized as names from the Bible. Names like Raphael, Michael, and Jehovah. Others meant nothing to me: Hagallatin, Zedeck, and Tetragrammaton. There were many strange symbols. Some looked Jewish but others bore no resemblance to anything I had ever seen before. The symbols were repeated, embroidered on the drapes and painted on what I had taken for a table but now saw to be an altar. The room reeked of incense . . . a sickly sweet smell that I was sure would linger long afterwards in my hair.

John busied himself with more of the stuff, sprinkling in onto glowing charcoal in an ornate incense-burner, which stood in the center of the altar.

"Is it all right to step within the circles?" I asked.

"Oh, yes," he replied. He smiled a crooked smile. "You won't get blasted by lightning, or anything. You see, it's consecrated only at the start of a ritual and then deconsecrated afterwards."

I still felt a little hesitant about it.

"Come along, colonel," said John. "Let's get this show on the road. You stand over here, in front of the altar."

Colonel Sumner shuffled into place and, drawing a little black book from his pocket, starting thumbing through it for the right place.

"Did you go through all this with Julie as well?" I asked, bitterly.

John looked surprised. "Good heavens, no!" he said. "She was simply Cynthia's secretary. She was cute and, regrettably, Cynthia took a dim view of my attentions to her."

"So you killed her!"

"Not before she had supplied some very interesting facts."

"What do you mean?"

"Facts concerning you, my love."

"Me?"

"Yes. That's why circumstances were 'maneuvered', shall we say, to bring you here. We had the devil of a job tracking you down in the first place too, I might add."

"I still don't understand." My head was spinning. Nothing made any sense.

"You don't have to," snapped John. "Let's just get on with it. Father! Take Rebecca's arm and stand by the door. When I give the signal – or when the Justice, here, gives the signal - you bring her to stand beside me. Understand?"

The old man seemed to get the idea and, clutching tightly to my arm, we moved to stand by the door.

"Ready, colonel?" asked John.

"Er – er, yes." The colonel seemed a trifle worried and tugged at his left ear.

Chapter Twenty-Five

My heat skipped a beat and I sensed John freeze. I had thought there was something vaguely familiar about the colonel, but I had not really studied him at all. My eyes locked on to those of the white-haired figure before the altar. Beneath the fake, white eyebrows those eyes were big and brown . . . and beautiful.

"Southwood!" cried John, in a strained voice.

Peter straightened up. "'Fraid so!" he said.

A good four inches shorter than John, Peter didn't move as the taller man advanced on him.

"I don't know what your game is," snarled John through clenched teeth. "But if you've got any ideas of playing the knight in shining armor, and rescuing the maiden in distress, I'd advise you to forget them."

He swung a fist at Peter but Peter was too quick. He ducked and slipped around so that the altar was between them. The thickening swirl of the incense smoke drifted up between the two men.

"What did you do with Babula"" John demanded.

"Oh, he' s safe enough . . . the authorities are taking good care of him. They'll be here, too, soon enough. They weren't far behind me."

John suddenly leapt forward and grabbed up the sword that had been lying on the altar. He swung it and I screamed when it just missed the top of Peter's head as he ducked down. The next minute it was John's turn to scream as Peter lunged against the altar, tipping it over and spilling red-hot charcoal from the censer on to John's legs.

"Wha' . . . wha' . . ."

I suddenly felt the old man, at my side, start to shake. I turned and saw that his eyes were wide and terrible. He let go of my arm and started hopping from one leg to the other, tearing at his hair. Saliva trickled from the corner of his mouth.

Oh, no, I thought! He's having a fit! I stepped away from him.

"John! John!" The old man's voice started to rise towards the high pitch of those soul-searing screams I'd heard so often.

"J-o-o-o-o-ohn!"

But John was unheeding, slashing wildly at Peter, who was only just managing to keep out of his range. In front of the window, John finally found his mark. A wild swing caught Peter as he slipped on the spilled wax from one of the black candles about the circle. I screamed again as I saw the wicked blade of the sword slash through Peter's sleeve, and saw the blood flow from an ugly gash in his arm.

"J-o-o-o-o-ohn!"

John's father suddenly rushed across the room to his son, screaming at the top of his voice. John – his mind only on the fight – was taken by surprise. He swung around, the sword raised as though to fend off fresh attackers. I screamed yet again as the blade went through the old man's body. I heard a crash of glass as darkness enveloped me and I fainted.

"She's coming around." It was Peter's voice.

I felt the soothing coolness of a damp towel against my forehead. I opened my eyes to find myself lying on the settee in the sitting room. Peter was perched on the edge of the seat beside me, anxiously looking down at me. Frau Brüning was hovering in the background. She looked as though she had been crying; something I had never thought her capable of.

"Becky? Are you okay? Can you hear me?"

I smiled up at Peter. "I'm fine," I said. "Stupid of me to faint."

Then I remembered the scene in the Magic Room up in the tower, with John slashing at Peter with his sword. I struggled to sit up.

"Your arm, Peter! How's your arm?"

He held me down, gently but firmly, with his left hand. I then saw that his right arm was heavily bandaged and in a sling. He was still dressed as the Justice of the Peace, though he had taken off the jacket plus the wig and make-up.

"My arm's fine," he said. "Frau Brüning has taken care of it. Now you just rest a bit. You've been through a terrible ordeal."

I sank back down again, not sorry to follow his advice.

"Peter," I said, after a moment. "What happened up there in the tower after I fainted? After that poor old man . . ."

"There!" he said, re-arranging the towel on my forehead. "Don't worry. Everything's okay now."

"Yes, but what happened? I thought I heard a crash."

"You did." He nodded. "When old man Fletcher charged across, and John skewered him, it knocked John backwards. The two of them crashed out through the window."

"Then, they're . . . ?"

"Dead. Yes."

We were both silent for a long moment.

"That old tower has certainly claimed its share of victims," I said.

Frau Brüning took up the bowl from the floor beside me and bustled off to the kitchen, saying she would make us some coffee. I sure felt I could use some.

"Are the police here yet, Peter?" I asked.

He nodded. "They're up in the tower now. And out at the foot of it. You'll see them later. I'm sure they'll want to ask questions."

"*They* will want to ask questions!" I laughed. "What about me? I've a few of my own."

"I can understand that."

Peter looked down at me and touched my cheek with his hand. It felt good. Warm, tender, and reassuring.

"What did John mean when he said I was an heiress?" I asked.

"Well, so you are. It's a long story but I'll give you the gist of it."

"I thought I was an orphan."

"No. Not really. When you were born your parents were very young and not long married. They had no money; your father had no job. They placed you in an orphanage because it was the only way they knew to make sure you got proper care . . . food and clothing. It broke their hearts to do it."

I felt a lump rising in my throat.

"There was a fire," Peter went on. "And all of the records were destroyed."

"I remember that," I said.

He nodded. "It seems you were one of only a handful who were saved. For years afterwards your parents didn't know whether you were alive or dead."

"I remember the orphanage named me Becky Valentine. What's my real name, Peter?"

"Rebecca Anne Wilmington," he said.

"Rebecca Anne Wilmington," I repeated. It had a nice ring to it . . . though I had grown fond of Valentine.

"Years later," Peter continued, "your father struck it rich. He invented an industrial chemical cleaner and went on to make a fortune. Of course, they tried to find you; to see if you were alive and where you had gone."

"That must have been some job," I said, struggling up into a sitting position. "I was shuffled from orphanage to orphanage; from foster home to foster home."

"Don't I know it," said Peter.

I raised an eyebrow.

"Your parents were killed last year," he said. "Your father's private jet crashed in the mountains outside Los Angeles. My boss was your father's lawyer. So *I* got the job of tracking you down."

"Now I'm beginning to see it," I said. "And Julie, who used to work in your office, let the story slip to John."

"Right! Unfortunately he managed to find you before I did."

"How did you manage to find me here?" I asked.

"Your old friend in Boston . . . Susan."

I was quiet for a moment. He took my hand and held it.

"So in one day I find my parents, after nearly twenty years, only to lose them again."

He nodded and squeezed my hand.

"How much am I worth, Peter?"

He smiled. "Rough estimate: a little over eight million."

I almost fainted again.

"Think you can handle it?" he asked.

I squeezed his hand.

"With the right lawyer," I said.

#

QUEEN VICTORIA PRESS

Books by Raymond Buckland

A MISTAKE THROUGH THE HEART   Book Three of the Bram Stoker Mysteries
    (books one and two published by Penguin's Berkley Prime Crime)

CHURCHILL'S SECRET SPY   World War Two espionage novel

THE PENNY COURT ENQUIRERS   Victorian mysteries series
    ONE CLUE AT A TIME   Book One
    THE NOBLE SAVAGE   Book Two
    DEADLY SPIRIT   Book Three

OUT OF THIS WORLD   A collection of science fiction short stories

PARANORMAL POETRY   A chapbook of poetry, strange and unusual

OUIJA CONNECTION TO SPIRIT   The talking board and how to contact the
    spirit world

WITCHCRAFT REVEALED   An examination of Witchcraft and Wicca

In Preparation:

THE WIITIKO INHERITANCE

THE SECRET LIFE OF MISS EMMELINE CROMWELL

Books by Eileen Lizzie Wells

FLETCHER'S FOLLY   A Gothic Romance Mystery

In Preparation:

THE POSTMISTRESS MYSTERIES

DESIGNING WOMEN

www.queenvictoriapress.com